IN THE
COUNTRY
OF MEN

IN THE
COUNTRY
OF MEN

———

Hisham Matar

THE DIAL PRESS

IN THE COUNTRY OF MEN
A Dial Press Book

Published by
The Dial Press
A Division of Random House, Inc.
New York, New York

Book design by Susan Turner

The Dial Press and Dial Press Trade Paperbacks are registered
trademarks of Random House, Inc., and the colophon is a
trademark of Random House, Inc.

ISBN-13: 978-0-7394-8400-5

Printed in the United States of America

IN THE
COUNTRY
OF MEN

1

I am recalling now that last summer before I was sent away. It was 1979, and the sun was everywhere. Tripoli lay brilliant and still beneath it. Every person, animal and ant went in desperate search for shade, those occasional gray patches of mercy carved into the white of everything. But true mercy only arrived at night, a breeze chilled by the vacant desert, moistened by the humming sea, a reluctant guest silently passing through the empty streets, vague about how far it was allowed to roam in this realm of the absolute star. And it was rising now, this star, as faithful as ever, chasing away the blessed breeze. It was almost morning.

The window in her bedroom was wide open, the glue tree outside it silent, its green shy in the early light. She hadn't fallen asleep until the sky was gray with dawn. And even then I was so rattled I couldn't leave her side, wondering if, like one of those hand puppets that play dead, she would bounce up again, light another cigarette and continue begging me, as she had been doing only minutes before, not to tell, not to tell.

Baba never found out about Mama's illness; she only fell ill when he was away on business. It was as if, when the world was empty of him, she and I remained as stupid reminders, empty pages that had to be filled with the memory of how they had come to be married.

I sat watching her beautiful face, her chest rise and fall with breath, unable to leave her side, hearing the things she had just told me swim and repeat in my head.

Eventually I left her and went to bed.

When she woke up she came to me. I felt her weight sink beside me, then her fingers in my hair. The sound of her fingernails on my scalp reminded me of once when I was unlucky. I had thrown a date in my mouth before splitting it open, only discovering it was infested with ants when their small shell bodies crackled beneath my teeth. I lay there silent, pretending to be asleep, listening to her breath disturbed by tears.

During breakfast I tried to say as little as possible. My silence made her nervous. She talked about what we might have for lunch. She asked if I would like some jam or honey. I said no, but she went to the fridge and got some anyway. Then, as was usual on the mornings after she had been ill, she took me on a drive to pull me out of my silence, to return me to myself again.

Waiting for the car to warm up, she turned on the radio, skipped through the dial and didn't stop until she heard the beautiful voice of Abd al-Basit Abd al-Sammad. I was glad because, as everyone knows, one must refrain from speaking and listen humbly to the Koran when it is read.

Just before we turned into Gergarish Street, the street

that follows the sea, Bahloul the beggar appeared out of nowhere. Mama hit the brakes and said *ya satir*. He wandered over to her side, walking slowly, clasping his dirty hands tightly to his stomach, his lips quivering. "Hello, Bahloul," Mama said, rummaging in her purse. "I see you, I see you," he said, and although these were the words Bahloul most often uttered, this time I thought what an idiot Bahloul is and wished he would just vanish. I watched him in the side mirror standing in the middle of the street, clutching the money Mama had given him to his chest like a man who has just caught a butterfly.

★

She took me downtown to the sesame man in the market by Martyrs' Square, the square that looked on to the sea, the square where a sculpture of Septimius Severus, the Roman emperor born all those years ago in Lepcis, proudly stood. She bought me as many sesame sticks as I wanted, each wrapped in white wax paper twisted at either end. I refused to let her put them in her bag. On such mornings I was always stubborn. "But I have some more shopping to do," she said. "You're bound to drop them like this." "No," I said, curling my eyebrows, "I'll wait for you outside," and walked off angrily, not caring if I lost her or became lost from her in the big city. "Listen," she called after me, attracting people's attention. "Wait for me by Septimius Severus."

There was a large café on one side that spilled out onto the passageway. Men, some faces I recognized from before, sat playing dominoes and cards. Their eyes were on Mama. I wondered if her dress shouldn't be looser.

As I walked away from her I felt my power over her recede; I began to feel sorry and sad how on such mornings she was always generous and embarrassed and shy, as if she had walked out naked. I wanted to run to her, to hold her hand, latch on to her dress as she shopped and dealt with the world, a world full of men and the greed of men. I forced myself not to look back and focused instead on the shops set within arched bays on either side of the covered passageway. Black silk scarves billowed gently above one, columns of stacked red caps stood as tall as men outside another. The ceiling was made with dark strips of fabric. The white blades of light that pierced through the occasional gaps illuminated the swimming dust and shone still and beautiful on the arches and floor, but darted like sparkles on the heads and down the bodies of the passersby, making the shadows seem much darker than they were.

Outside, the square was flooded with sunlight. The ground was almost white with brightness, making the dark shoes and figures crossing it look like things floating above the world. I wished I had left the sesame sticks with her. Small needles were now pricking my arms. I told myself off for being stubborn and for letting her buy me so many. I looked at them in my arms and felt no appetite for them.

I leaned against the cool marble pedestal of Septimius Severus. The Roman emperor stood above me, his silver-studded belt curving below his belly, pointing his arm toward the sea, "Urging Libya to look toward Rome," was how Ustath Rashid described the pose. Ustath Rashid taught art history at el-Fateh University and was my best friend Kareem's father. I remembered our Guide standing in one of his military uniforms like this, waving his arm as the tanks passed in front of him on Revolution Day.

I turned toward the sea, the shining turquoise sea beyond the square. It seemed like a giant blue monster rising at the

edge of the world. "Grrr," I growled, then wondered if anyone had heard me. I kicked my heel against the pedestal several times. I stared at the ground, into the heat and
brightness that made me want to sleep with my eyes open.
But then, not looking for but falling directly on my target, I
spotted Baba.

He was standing on the edge of the pavement in a street
opposite the square, looking both ways for traffic, arching
forward as if he was about to fall. Before he stepped on to
the road he motioned with his hand then snapped his fingers
twice. It was a gesture that I knew. Sometimes he would
wave to me like that, as if to say, "Come on, come on," then
snap his fingers, "Hey, wake up." Behind him appeared
Nasser, Baba's office clerk, carrying a small shiny black
typewriter beneath his arm, struggling to keep up. Baba was
already crossing the street, walking toward me. For a moment I thought he might be bringing Nasser to Septimius
Severus, to teach him all the things he had taught me about
the Roman emperor, Lepcis Magna and Rome. For Baba regarded Nasser as a younger brother; he often said so himself.

"Baba?" I whispered.

Two dark lenses curved like the humpbacks of turtles
over his eyes. The sky, the sun and the sea were painted by
God in colors we could all point at and say the sea is
turquoise, the sun banana, the sky blue. Sunglasses are terrible, I thought, because they change all of this and keep those
who wear them at a distance. At that moment I remembered
how, only a couple of days ago, he had kissed us good-bye.
"May God bring you back safely," Mama told him, "and
make your trip profitable." I had kissed his hand like he
taught me to. He had leaned down and whispered in my ear,

"Take care of your mother, you are the man of the house now," and grinned at me in the way people do when they think they have paid you a compliment. But look now, look; walking where I could touch him, here where we should be together. My heart quickened. He was coming closer. Maybe he means me, I thought. It was impossible to see his eyes.

I watched him walk in that familiar way—his head pointing up slightly, his polished leather shoes flicking ahead with every step—hoping he would call my name, wave his hand, snap his fingers. I swear if he had I would have leaped into his arms. When he was right there, close enough that if I extended my arm I could touch him, I held my breath and my ears filled with silence. I watched his solemn expression—an expression I admired and feared—caught the scent-edge of his cologne, felt the air swell around him as he walked past. He was immediately followed by Nasser, carrying the black shiny typewriter under one arm. I wished I was him, following Baba like a shadow. They entered one of the buildings overlooking the square. It was a white building with green shutters. Green was the color of the revolution, but you rarely saw shutters painted in it.

"Didn't I tell you to wait by the sculpture?" I heard Mama say from behind me. I looked back and saw that I had strayed far from Septimius Severus.

★

I felt sick, anxious that I had somehow done the wrong thing. Baba wasn't on a business trip, but here, in Tripoli, where we should be together. I could have reached out and caught him from where he was heading; why had I not acted?

I sat in the car while she loaded the shopping, still holding on to the sesame sticks. I looked up at the building Baba and Nasser had entered. A window on the top floor shuddered, then swung open. Baba appeared through it. He gazed at the square, no longer wearing the sunglasses, leaning with his hands on the sill like a leader waiting for the clapping and chanting to stop. He hung a small red towel on the clothesline and disappeared inside.

★

On the way home I was more silent than before, and this time there was no effort in it. As soon as we left Martyrs' Square Mama began craning her neck toward the rearview mirror. Stopping at the next traffic light, she whispered a prayer to herself. A car stopped so close beside us I could have touched the driver's cheek. Four men dressed in dark safari suits sat looking at us. At first I didn't recognize them, then I remembered. I remembered so suddenly I felt my heart jump. They were the same Revolutionary Committee men who had come a week before and taken Ustath Rashid.

Mama looked ahead, her back a few centimeters away from the backrest, her fists tight around the steering wheel. She released one hand, brought it to my knee and sternly whispered, "Face forward."

When the traffic light turned green, the car beside us didn't move. Everyone knows you mustn't overtake a Revolutionary Committee car, and if you have to, then you must do it discreetly, without showing any pleasure in it. A few cars, unaware of who was parked beside us, began to sound their horns. Mama drove off slowly, looking more at the rearview mirror than the road ahead. Then she said, "They are following us; don't look back." I stared at my bare knees and said the same prayer over and over. I felt the sweat gather between my palms and the wax-paper wrapping of the sesame sticks.

It wasn't until we were almost home that Mama said, "OK, they are gone," then mumbled to herself, "Nothing better to do than give us an escort, the rotten rats."

My heart eased and my back grew taller. The prayer left my lips.

The innocent, Sheikh Mustafa, the imam of our local mosque, had told me, have no cause to fear; only the guilty live in fear.

★

I didn't help her carry the shopping into the house as was usual. I went straight to my room and dropped the sesame sticks on the bed, shaking the blood back into my arms. I grabbed my picture book on Lepcis Magna. Ten days before I had visited the ancient city for the first and, as it turned out, last time. Images of the deserted city of ruins by the sea still lingered vividly in my mind. I longed to return to it.

I didn't come out until I had to: after she had prepared lunch and set the table and called my name.

When she tore the bread, she handed me a piece; and I, noticing she hadn't had any salad, passed her the salad bowl. Midway through the meal she got up and turned on the radio. She left it on a man talking about farming the desert. I got up, said, "Bless your hands," and went to my room. "I will take a nap," she said after me. My silence made her say things she didn't need to say, she always took a nap in the afternoons, everyone did, everyone except me. I never could nap.

I waited in my room until she had finished washing the dishes and putting away the food, until I was certain she had gone to sleep, then I came out.

I was walking around the house looking for something to

do when the telephone rang. I ran to it before it could wake her up. It was Baba. On hearing his voice my heart quickened. I thought he must be calling so soon after I had seen him to explain why he hadn't greeted me.

"Where are you?"

"Abroad. Let me speak to your mother."

"Where abroad?"

"Abroad," he repeated, as if it was obvious where that was. "I'll be home tomorrow."

"I miss you."

"Me too. Call your mother."

"She's asleep. Shall I wake her up?"

"Just let her know I'll be home tomorrow, about lunch-time."

I didn't want the conversation to end so I said, "We were followed today by that same white car that took Ustath Rashid. We were side by side at the traffic light and I saw their faces. I was so close I could have touched the driver's cheek and I wasn't frightened. Not at all. Not even a little, I wasn't."

"I'll see you tomorrow," he said and hung up.

I stood for a while beside the telephone and listened to the thick silence that seemed to descend on our house during those hours in the afternoon, a silence edged by the humming of the fridge in the kitchen and the ticking of the clock in the hallway.

I went to watch Mama sleep. I sat beside her, checking first that her chest was rising and falling with breath. I remembered the words she had told me the night before, "We are two halves of the same soul, two open pages of the same book," words that felt like a gift I didn't want.

2

I was woken up in the middle of the night by the sound of glass shattering. A light was on in the kitchen. Mama was on her knees, talking to herself and collecting pieces of glass from the floor. She was barefoot. When she saw me she covered her mouth with the inside of her wrist, her cupped hand full of broken glass, and giggled that strange nervous giggle that was somewhere between laughter and crying. I ran to fetch her slippers, then threw them to her, but she shook her head and stumbled over to the rubbish bin and emptied her hand. She began sweeping the floor. When the broom reached the slippers she paused then put them on.

I could see her medicine bottle half empty on the breakfast table. There was no glass beside it, just a cigarette burning in an ashtray littered with butts and black-headed matchsticks. Her glass must have shattered. Mama was ill again. I felt my cheeks burn with anger: where is Baba? He should be here because when he's home everything is nor-

mal, she is never ill and I am never woken up like this to find
everything changed.

She sat down, stood up again, fetched another glass and
filled it with medicine. The kitchen reeked of it. The smell
made my head heavy. She turned to me. I was still standing
in the doorway of the kitchen. She giggled again, asked,
"What?" and rolled her eyes away. "What's the matter with
you? Why are you staring at me like that? Have you got
nothing better to do?" She shook her head to herself. "I
don't know why you are looking at me like that. I haven't
done anything." Then with an exaggerated earnestness she
said, "Go back to bed, it's late."

I went back to bed but couldn't sleep. I heard her go into
the bathroom. She was there for a long time. I didn't hear
any water running. My heart began to race. Then suddenly
she came out and went to her room. I walked to her door,
then hesitated.

"Hello, habibi," she said. "What's the matter, can't
sleep?"

I shook my head to say no, happy to play her game, to
pretend that some bad dream had broken my sleep. She patted the bed and I lay beside her. Just when sleep was curling
itself around me, she started her telling. Her mouth beside
my ear, the smell of her medicine alive in the room.

★

The only things that mattered were in the past. And what
mattered the most in the past was how she and Baba came
to be married, that "black day," as she called it. She never
started the story from the beginning; like Scheherazade she
didn't move in a straight line but jumped from one episode
to another, leaving questions unanswered, questions the

asking of which I feared would interrupt her telling. I had to restrain myself and try to remember every piece of the story in the hope that one day I could fit it all into a narrative that was straight and clear and simple. For although I feared those nights when we were alone and she was ill, I never wanted her to stop talking. Her story was mine too, it bound us, turned us into one, "two halves of the same soul, two open pages of the same book," as she used to say.

Once she began by saying, "You are my prince. One day you'll be a man and take me away on your white horse." She placed her palms on my cheeks, her eyes brimming with tears. "And I almost didn't . . . You are my miracle. The pills, all the other ways in which I tried to resist. I didn't know you were going to be so beautiful, fill my heart . . ." This is why I often lay in my darkened bedroom dreaming of saving her.

When Mama heard that her father had found her a groom, she swallowed a "handful of magic pills." "They called them that," she said, "because they made a woman no good. For who would want to remain married to a woman who couldn't bear children? In a few months, I thought, a year at the most, I'll be free to resume my schooling. It was a perfect plan, or so I thought.

"They rushed the wedding through as if I was a harlot, as if I was pregnant and had to be married off before it showed. Part of the punishment was not to allow me even to see a photograph of my future husband. But the maid sneaked in to tell me she had seen the groom. 'Ugly,' she said, frowning, 'big nose,' then spat at the ground. I was so frightened. I ran to the toilet ten times or more. My father and brothers—the High Council, who were sitting right out-side the room—became more and more nervous, reading my weak stomach as proof of my crime. They didn't know how it felt waiting in that room, where the complete stranger who was now my husband was going to walk in alone and, without introduction, undress me and do filthy, revolting things.

"It was a dreary room. It had nothing in it but a huge bed with a square, ironed white handkerchief on one pillow. I had no idea what the handkerchief was for.

"I walked up and down that room in my wedding dress wondering what kind of a face my executioner had. Because that's how I saw it: they passed the judgment and he, the stranger armed with the marriage contract signed by my father, was going to carry out the punishment. When he touches me, which I was sure he was going to do, there will be no point in screaming; I was his right, his wife under God. I was only fourteen but I knew what a man had to do to his wife. Cousin Khadija, a chatterbox who had fallen as silent as a wall after her wedding night, had later, when she and I were alone, told me how her husband had lost patience with her and with his fingers punctured her veil and bled her. It was the duty of every man to prove his wife a virgin."

I didn't know what Mama meant, but feared that when the time came I might not have what it takes to "puncture" a woman.

"Betrayal was a hand squeezing my throat," she continued. "Those hours seemed eternal. My stomach churned, my fingers were as cold as ice cubes, and my hands wrestled with each other.

"On one of my journeys to the toilet, pulling my wedding dress up and running like an idiot, I saw my father bury a pistol in his pocket. 'Blood is going to be spilled either way,' were the words he told your grandmother. She told me this later, almost laughing, relieved, giddy and ridiculous with happiness. 'If, God forbid,' she had said, 'you didn't turn out virtuous and true, your father was prepared to take your life.'

"Your father, the mystery groom, was twenty-three; to the fourteen-year-old girl I was that seemed ancient. When he finally walked in, I fainted. When I came to, he wasn't there. Your grandfather was beside me, smiling, your grandmother behind him, clutching the now bloodstained handkerchief to her chest and crying with happiness.

"I was sick for days. The stupid pills didn't work. I took too many and all that vomiting squeezed them out of me. Nine months later I had you."

★

The medicine changed her eyes and made her lose her balance. Sometimes even before seeing her I could tell she was ill. I would come into the house and notice a certain stillness, something altered. I knew without knowing how I knew, like that one time when, playing football with the boys, one of Osama's mighty strikes had hit me in the back of the head and I was knocked out. Just before it happened I remember seeing Kareem's face trying to warn me, then I listened to that strange silence fill my ears. This felt the same. I could be reading in my room or playing in our street, and that quiet anxiety would visit me. I would call out for her even though I didn't need her. And when I saw her eyes lost in her face and heard her voice, that strange nervous giggle, I was certain that Mama was ill again. Sometimes I felt the panic, then found her well, immersed in a book by Nizar al-Qabbani, her favorite poet. That upset me more.

When she was ill, she would talk and talk and talk but

later hardly remember any of what she had told me. It was as if her illness got the spirit of another woman in her.

In the morning, after I had fallen asleep exhausted from listening to her craziness and from guarding her—afraid she would burn herself or leave the gas on in the kitchen or, God forbid, leave the house altogether and bring shame and talk down on us—she would come and sit beside me, comb my hair with her fingers and apologize and sometimes even cry a little. I would then be stung by her breath, heavy with medicine, unable to frown or turn my face because I wanted her to believe I was in a deep sleep.

She was shocked when I repeated to her the things she had told me the night before. "Who told you this?" she would ask. "You," I would shout—shout because I was unable not to. Then she would look away and say, "You shouldn't have heard that."

Sometimes she talked about Scheherazade. *A Thousand and One Nights* had been her mother's favorite story, and although my grandmother couldn't read she had memorized the entire book, word for word, and recited it regularly to her children. When I was first told this, I dreamed of my grandmother, whom I rarely saw, struggling to swallow the entire book. Nothing angered Mama more than the story of Scheherazade. I had always thought Scheherazade a brave woman who had gained her freedom through inventing tales and often, in moments of great fear, recalled her example.

"You should find yourself another model," Mama once began. "Scheherazade was a coward who accepted slavery over death. You know the closing chapter? 'The Marriage of King Shahryar and Scheherazade'? When she finally, after having lived with him for God knows how long, after sleeping with him—nothing, of course, is ever said of that—bearing

him not one, not two, but three sons, after all of that she managed to gather her courage, your *brave* Scheherazade, to finally ask the question: 'May I be so bold as to ask a favor of
Your Highness?' And what was this favor that she was pleading to be so bold as to ask? What was it?" Mama shouted, her
eyes not leaving me. "Was it to rule one of the corners or even
a dirty little cave in his kingdom? Was it to be given one of the
ministries? Perhaps a school? Or was it to be given a writing
desk in a quiet room in his palace of endless rooms, a room
the woman could call her own, to write in secret the truth of
this monster Shahryar? No. She gathered her children around
her—'one walking, one crawling and one sucking,' as the
book tells us. All sons, of course. I wonder how successful she
would have been if they were three harlots like her."

What scared me the most during such nights was how
different Mama became. She said words in front of me that
made my cheeks blush and my heart shudder. Saliva gathered at the corners of her lips. She didn't look beautiful anymore.

"Your heroine's boldness was to ask to be allowed to . . . ?"
She held the word in the air, staring at me, casting her hand
slowly in a curve as if she was presenting a feast. "To live."

Her eyes fixed on me, expecting me to say something, to
be outraged, to slap my thigh, sigh, click my tongue and
shake my head. I faced my lap, pretending to be busy with
something between my fingers, hoping the moment would
pass. And when she started speaking again I was always relieved that her voice had come to fill the void.

"To live," she repeated. "And not because she had as
much right to live as he, but because if he were to kill her, his
sons would live 'motherless.'" Mama covered her mouth
with the back of her hand and giggled like a child. "'Release

me,' your Scheherazade begged, 'release me from the doom
of death as a dole to these infants. You will find nobody
among all the women in your realm to raise them as they
should be raised.' Stupid harlot. My guess: five, maybe ten
years at the most before she got the sword. As soon as the
'one sucking' became the 'one walking' and her muscles,
Scheherazade's fine, supple muscles . . ." Mama said, frowning in disgust. The ceiling light seemed too harsh on her
face. I wondered if I should switch it off, switch on the side
lamps instead. "Those so important for pleasing the king,
the mighty, the majestic Shahryar, had loosened . . ." Her
eyes were wet now, her lower lip quivered slightly. "As soon
as she was no longer tempting, useful; as soon as she was no
longer beautiful: whack! Gone with the head," she said and
then her own head dropped and her legs extended before
her. I thought she was going to fall off the sofa, but she remained still, silent for a couple of minutes. I imagined how it
might be to live without her. A warm swirl spun in my belly,
something warm and dependable gripped my heart and sent
a rush through me. I wasn't sure if it was fear or excitement
that I felt at the thought of losing her. Then she seemed to
wake up. She looked at me as if it was the first time we had
met. She scanned the room, paused for a moment, then lit a
cigarette. "You should go to bed," she said, looking away.

★

On the mornings after she was always nice. She liked to take
me out driving. If it was a school day she would ask,
"Anything important today?" I would shrug my shoulders
and she would say, "I'll telephone the school and tell them
you're not well." In the car she talked a lot and wasn't surprised by my silence. She didn't mind stopping under the

pedestrian bridge that crossed over Gorgi Street so I could watch the bad boys hanging above the fast traffic by their arms and some, the truly brave ones, by their ankles. Normally, when we passed under them, she would ask me to shut my eyes. But on such mornings she was happy to park beside them and let me watch. Sometimes she would even say, "I must admit, they are quite brave." Then, "Promise you would never do that. Promise you would always protect yourself." Sometimes I nodded and sometimes I didn't.

On some mornings she took me all the way to town just to buy sesame sticks. Or, if she had been very ill the night before, she would take me to Signor Il Calzoni's restaurant by the sea, in Gergarish, for grilled shrimp and spaghetti. In winter I ordered the beet-and-tomato soup with bread and cheese and bresaola. I liked the way the beet painted my spit and tongue purple for hours.

Signor Il Calzoni had a big machine that squeezed oranges all on its own and he would take me to push the button that set the whole thing working, cutting oranges and squeezing them in front of you. I didn't like orange juice that much but some days I drank up to five glasses just to watch the thing work. After the meal I always got gelati. Mama ordered cappuccino and sipped it slowly, looking out on to the sea, squinting her eyes at the horizon where on a clear day we could see Malta, a giant biscuit floating on the sea.

Signor Il Calzoni was always pleased to see us. He would take us to our table by the window and hover in search of conversation. He spoke about how much he missed Italy and how much he loved Libya. And occasionally he would chant, loud enough for all in the restaurant to hear, "Long live the Guide," toward a large mural he had had a couple of art students paint at one end of the restaurant. It showed the

Colonel in his full military uniform, curling his eyebrows and looking very serious. And if the restaurant had a table of Revolutionary Committee men, or Mokhabarat, people we called Antennae, he chanted, "El-Fateh, el-Fateh, el-Fateh," punching the air with his fist until the waiters joined in. Sometimes the chef too came out and I got to see his tall, puffy white hat.

The things she told me pressed down on my chest, so heavy that it seemed impossible to carry on living without spilling them. I didn't want to break my promise—the promise she always forced me to give, sometimes over thirty times in one night, not to tell, to swear on her life, again and again, and then be warned, "If you tell a living soul and I die, my life will be on your neck"—so I tried to tell her. We were at Signor Il Calzoni's restaurant. She kept interrupting me, pleading with me to stop. So I covered my ears, shut my eyes and spoke like a robot above her. She slapped the table and said, "Please, Suleiman, I beg you, don't embarrass me," and whispered sternly through flexed lips, "A boy your age should never speak such things." Then she changed her tone and said, "Habibi, light of my eyes, promise you won't tell anyone. Especially Moosa. I know how much you love him, but nothing ever stays in that man's mouth. Promise." I nodded, wrapping my arms around myself, doubling over: this was the only way I could keep it all inside.

Signor Il Calzoni avoided coming to our table when he saw us like this. He would stand beside his cashier, pretending not to look.

Sometimes I couldn't get myself to eat, and Mama would think I was punishing her. "What do you want from me?" she would whisper angrily across the table. "I have given up everything for you. You're not even satisfied."

If I began to cry, Signor Il Calzoni would take me to squeeze more oranges, holding my hand and talking in his funny accent. Then, if the restaurant was completely empty, he would sit beside me, look out on to the sea and say, "Ah. Look how beautiful your country is, Suleiman. Now it's mine too, no? I am also Libyan, like you. I speak like a Libyan, no?" "No," I would say just to make him laugh. He had a wonderful laugh. His entire body would bounce beside me. The seats were spring-upholstered and so I would do the same. And that made him blush in front of Mama. "You should change your name from Signor Il Calzoni to Signor al-Husseini." That always made him bounce.

On the way home I regretted all the talking and laughing, regretted breaking my silence, allowing myself to be tricked like a cat teased out from beneath a bed with a string. I knew I had failed when, on our way back home, late in the afternoon when the bread was no longer at its best, she would stop by the empty bakery. I would stand to one side, pretending to be drawing shapes with my sandal into the flour-dusted floor, and watch the baker Majdi reach beneath his deep counter and think, that's the devil. He would hand her a bottle wrapped in a black plastic bag, and she would immediately bury it in her handbag. And when we were in the car she didn't place her bag beside her as she normally did, but beneath her legs, well out of view. I knew it was her medicine, bad for her and bad for me, but, doubtful of the world and my place in it, I said nothing. I massacred the hardened ends of each loaf and she didn't complain that I was ruining them.

★

Mama and I spent most of the time together—she alone, I unable to leave her. I worried how the world might change if even for a second I was to look away, to relax the grip of my gaze. I was convinced that if my attention was applied fully, disaster would be kept at bay and she would return whole and uncorrupted, no longer lost, stranded on the opposite bank, waiting alone. But although her unpredictability and her urgent stories tormented me, my vigil and what I then could only explain as her illness bound us into an intimacy that has since occupied the innermost memory I have of love. If love starts somewhere, if it is a hidden force that is brought out by a person, like light off a mirror, for me that person was her. There was anger, there was pity, even the dark warm embrace of hate, but always love and always the joy that surrounds the beginning of love.

3

That summer Ustath Rashid taught his son how to drive. He would prop Kareem up on a pillow and let him drive around the quiet streets of Gergarish. A week before we went to Lepcis, Kareem took his father's car keys without asking permission and drove me to the sea. He tried to get as close to the water as possible, but as soon as we reached the shore the wheels sank into the sand.

"Why won't you come to Lepcis?"

"Mama won't let me."

"Stop making excuses. She already told Baba you can. What are you afraid of?"

"I am not afraid." He didn't seem convinced. I worried he would think me a mommy's boy, so I told him. "She's ill," I said. "I think she will die soon."

"But all women are ill," Kareem said. "Mama bleeds all the time."

"Really?"

"Yes. Sometimes I go into the bathroom and find the toilet water red. It's disgusting. It's their curse. But don't worry, it doesn't mean they will die."

The sea was as flat and still as oil. We ran until the water tripped us. We raced toward the turquoise, where the deep sea was cooler. I felt bad for Kareem, but also relieved that at least my mother didn't bleed.

"You'll love Lepcis." He dived and tickled my feet.

Back on land we collected stones, wood and any rubbish we could find to stuff behind the wheels. The engine moaned and the car shifted sideways before it wriggled its way out of the sand.

★

Kareem had been to Lepcis Magna several times with his father. He had also seen Ghadames and Sabratha, the cave paintings in Fezzan. He had even been on a boat to Crete, where he said women swam naked. Like me, he was an only child. This was very rare because parents with only one offspring were always at risk of leading people to believe that either the woman was no longer good, or, God forbid, both the mother and the father were objecting to God's Will. Mama was often asked why she didn't have more children. She would blush at the question. Baba blushed too when he was nudged by a friend and asked in a whisper why he didn't take another wife. Maybe it was this that in spite of the age difference—Kareem was twelve, where I was nine— had brought us close to each other. Because what united Kareem and me rarely felt like friendship, but something like blood or virtue. I wanted so much to be like him.

When Kareem and his parents first moved in next door, Mama went to pay them a visit. She asked me to put on my black leather shoes, which I hardly wore because they were heavy and scraped against my ankles, and she ironed my white shirt and insisted I button its collar. I didn't mind because I was eager to meet my new next-door neighbor, who, the boys in the street had told me, was like me, without brother or sister. But when we arrived, his mother, Auntie Salma, said that Kareem had gone out with his father to explore the area, then smiled, tilted her head to one side and said, "Sorry."

Our street was mostly lined with building plots, the foundations dug up and abandoned. The only five completed houses, identical in design, huddled together in the center of the street: ours and Kareem's on one side; the other three, where Adnan, Masoud and Ali and Osama lived, on the opposite side.

I wandered around our new neighbors' house, amused by the strangeness of being in a building that was the mirror image of ours on the outside but on the inside was completely altered by the different furniture and the colors of the walls: like two brothers who had grown distant. Our walls were lined in Italian wallpaper, European flowers in full bloom, autumn leaves falling always, the same bird perched on top of the same branch and plucking at the same twig over and over again, foreign butterflies on armchairs, tables in dark, satisfied woods and our windows dressed in Dutch cloth and French velvet. Their walls were painted pastel, the baseboards a dark brown, "So that when they get dirty it won't show," Auntie Salma explained, showing Mama around the house. "What a clever idea," Mama said, with worrying enthusiasm. Their windows were covered in the same cotton fabric, the sort of thing that was commonly found in Libya then, imported from Egypt. They weren't as well off as we were; Ustath Rashid was only a university professor, whereas Baba was a businessman who traveled the world looking for beautiful things and animals and trees to bring to our country. That night I thanked God for our wealth and asked him to keep us so forever and ever.

★

A couple of days before Ustath Rashid was taken I joined him, his students and Kareem on a day trip to Lepcis. I felt a string in my heart break as I looked back at Mama waving good-bye. Baba wasn't home.

At the beginning of the trip I was nervous, but then the whole bus began singing and clapping. Ustath Rashid's students were wonderfully jubilant; watching them I burned with anticipation to be at university. A couple of girls were pulled up to dance. With eyes downcast they shook their hips and twirled their hands in the air. Passing cars blew their horns. We were like a wedding party.

Kareem and I were sitting in the back, Ustath Rashid in the front, occasionally looking back at us and smiling. When the dancing and the clapping subsided, a chant took hold: "al-Doctor, al-Doctor, al-Doctor" . . . We didn't stop until Ustath Rashid stood up and turned to face us.

"I am truly honored to have such an orderly, well-mannered and respectable group of students. I would just like to know where you unruly bunch have hidden them."

We all laughed, clapping and whistling as loudly as we could.

"The city of Lepcis Magna was founded by people from Tyre . . ."

"LEBANON."

"Yes—very good—modern-day Lebanon. Subsequently

it became Phoenician, then, of course, Roman, when it was made famous by its loyal son, Emperor Sep . . ."

"SEPTIMIUS SEVERUS."

"Yes, our Grim African, both a source of pride and shame."

"PRIDE, PRIDE."

"Well, if you insist."

Then the bus turned down a dirt road that led to the sea.

"Welcome to Lepcis," Ustath Rashid announced.

He seemed transformed. Stepping down from the bus, smiling at the abandoned city scattered by the lapping sea, its twisted columns like heavy sleeping giants by the shore, he gave a deep sigh and recited a poem:

Why this emptiness after joy?
Why this ending after glory?
Why this nothingness where once was a city?
Who will answer? Only the wind
Which steals the chantings of priests
And scatters the souls once gathered.

Some of his students clapped. He smiled, bowed, his cheeks blushing.

"Sidi Mahrez's lamentation for Carthage could have equally applied to Lepcis," he said, marching ahead.

We all struggled to keep up.

He took us to see a broken frieze that displayed part of the emperor's name. Absence was everywhere. Arches stood without the walls and roofs of the shops they had once belonged to and seemed, in the empty square under the open sky, like old men trying to remember where they were going. Coiled ivy and clusters of grapes were carved into their stone. White-stone-cobbled streets—some heading toward the sea, others into the surrounding green desert—marched bravely into the rising sand that erased them. Ferns, grass and wild sage shot through the stone-paved floor. Palm trees bowed like old gossiping women at the edges of the city.

He showed us the Medusa medallions carved in marble and inset high between the leap and dive of the limestone arches. They were boys with healthy cheeks full as moons, encircled with lush curls, their foreheads flexed, eyes anxiously inspecting the distance, lips gently open. "They are also known as the sea monsters," Ustath Rashid said, "always facing the sea, always expecting the worst."

Kareem continued staring up at the Medusa medallions long after the group had wandered off to the next object.

"What's the point?" he said.

"To scare away the enemy," I said.

"And how do you expect them to do that?"

"I don't know," I said and walked away.

"Children are useless in a war," he said, following me.

We caught up with Ustath Rashid in what were the baths, tiled rectangular cubes carved into the ground and under domed roofs. Flaked frescoes of men stabbing spears into the necks of lions and cheetahs, others on boats in a river full of yawning fish, lined the walls and ceilings. Ustath Rashid stopped in front of a painting of a naked woman.

"This is a maenad, a follower of the cult of Dionysus, the god that alleviates inhibitions and inspires creativity."

Her eyes were as strange as a bird's, her lips full and melancholy, the area around her nipples glowed pink, and her stomach stretched down to hips that widened out softly. She was dancing, one hand above her head, the other out by her waist. I could hear Ustath Rashid's voice going further, footsteps following him. I came closer to her, traced my

finger around the dark swirl of her belly button. I turned
my finger around the pink center of her nipple. Then my
eyes fell on her dark lips. I kissed them, hearing my own
breath against the cool dry stone. Something like guilt or
fear made me withdraw. I felt a swirl of excitement in my
belly. Her eyes seemed to be looking at me. I quickly kissed
her again and ran to catch up with the others.

We picnicked there, and when everyone was lying under
trees resting, Kareem and I went exploring. We spotted two
of Ustath Rashid's students hugging below a chestnut tree.
We watched him slip his hand beneath her jumper. She
moaned a strange moan. Later the man got in a fistfight with
another student. We weren't sure if it was over the girl.
When one punched the other in the face it didn't sound like
it did in the films; instead of a bang it was more like a wet
kiss. Ustath Rashid put himself between them and got his
spectacles knocked off. Everyone fell silent then. He smiled
strangely while he searched for his spectacles. They all
watched him. Kareem spotted them in the dirt and picked
them up. He placed them in his father's hand. Ustath Rashid
fixed them over his ears and smiled again, facing the ground,
as if it was he who had lost his temper and was now embarrassed.

Just when everybody was preparing to leave, Kareem
took me to see the amphitheater. We took turns running
down to the stage to hear our voices amplified against the
rising steps shaped in a crescent moon. By this time thick
clouds were drifting into the sky, black and bruised. The sea
was growing louder, crashing against the shore, then the
rain fell.

On the way back most of the bus was asleep. I watched
Kareem nuzzle into his father's side.

★

At times I used to wish that Baba was more like Ustath Rashid. The two men were good friends, if unalike. Baba was much more aloof. The times I felt closest to him were when he was unaware of my presence: watching him spread his library of neckties on the bed, for example, humming an unfamiliar tune. Even the way he swam seemed distant: floating on his back, his toes pointing to the sky, his eyes shut, unconcerned where the waters might take him. At home he was often busy with a book or the endless number of newspapers that appeared at our door every morning. I would sometimes curl up beside him, but his powers of concentration were amazing and he would hardly notice me. I would study his face as he read. Even the English mints he bought on his trips abroad, and which he kept in a small silver box, seemed mysterious: they were the size of small aspirin pills, but as soon as I put one in my mouth it set it on fire. He would sometimes say something in Italian at the newspaper. That always made Mama laugh. "Your father is swearing at the paper," she would say.

Although he traveled more than Ustath Rashid he never took me with him. I begged him several times and once I felt so sick with sadness that I screamed, kicked his shins and pummeled his thighs, and, when Mama restrained me, I cried and called him "Ugly!" He drove off just the same. I never again asked him to take me with him or cried in front of him when he came to leave.

At other times I secretly wished that Moosa, Baba's closest friend, was my father instead. Moosa was much younger, closer to Mama's age, and as tall as a tree. He often carried me on his shoulders to pick the high fruit, sweetened by the sun, on the crowns of the plum and orange trees in our garden.

★

Once Baba returned from one of his business trips with a huge open truck full of trees that had come by sea from Sweden. It was strange to have them sleep outside our house. They were dark and moist and smelled like human skin. Mama and I spread the atlas on the kitchen table to see where exactly Sweden was and by which sea route Baba's trees had come. Another time the truck was full of cows, black and dark brown from Scotland. We—Baba, Mama, Moosa and I—fed them without letting them off the truck, stuffing the feed through the fence, their round big black glassy eyes following us in silence. Mama sang to them the way she sang to herself when she was in the bathroom, or when she was hanging clothes on the clothesline in the garden, softly like a little girl unaware of herself. Baba walked around the truck several times, making sure each cow got its share. The cows were silent the whole time, chewing gloomily.

I spent the whole of that day unable to leave them alone, turning around the truck, looking up at their pink titties, climbing to stare into their peculiar eyes. After naptime the boys came out and began teasing them too. Masoud wiggled his bum at them and mooed, causing his brother Ali to laugh so hard a vein on either side of his tiny neck bulged out. Osama wanted to hear them moo so he threw a couple of stones at them and the cows huddled together, their sudden movement causing the truck to rock slightly. This seemed to awaken a new fear in Ali; he ran to his front door and stood frowning at his fingers. "Come, don't be such a baby," his brother Masoud said. Ali ran inside his house and didn't come out for the rest of the day. When I threatened Osama I would tell Baba, he sighed and dropped the stones in his hands.

By nightfall the cows began to moo.

"Maybe they are frightened," I suggested.

Moosa said it was the heat that bothered them. "Where they are from the sun has no heat and barely any light," he said.

"So you want to convince us you've been to Scotland?" Mama told him.

"No. I saw it in a film. I felt a chill just watching it."

Baba couldn't say how cold Scotland was because he had bought the cows off a man in Malta, which was only across the sea.

The following morning, after Baba had driven off with them, Um Masoud came to our door to complain. She was Masoud and Ali's mother and lived in the house across the street from ours. Like her two sons, Um Masoud was fat. Her buttocks were the size of giant watermelons. Although I never tried it, of course, I was certain I could balance a glass of water on one of them. Holding her youngest, Ali, by one hand and waving the other beside her ear, she said, "I can still hear their mooing and suspect I will for a long time to come. Ali couldn't even sleep." Ali was only six and, standing beside his huge mother, he looked like a dwarf. I stuck my tongue out at him. He frowned and looked away. "He woke up several times screaming. And this is to say nothing of the stink they left behind in our street."

"You just have," Mama murmured.

"What did you say?" Um Masoud said, suspicion forcing her eyebrows into a deep V.

"Nothing," Mama said.

Um Masoud walked away, pulling Ali by the hand, and repeating, "Cows? Cows in our street?"

"Next time we will import snakes," Mama said under her breath. "Silent, odorless snakes."

"What would people say?" Um Masoud continued. "That we bring cows into our homes? It's not normal, this."

I was glad she hadn't heard what Mama said about the snakes. Um Masoud's husband, Ustath Jafer, was an Antenna, a man of the Mokhabarat, "able to put people behind the sun," as I had heard it said many times.

★

Two days after we returned from Lepcis, and a week before I had seen Baba walk across Martyrs' Square, Ustath Rashid was taken.

I had seen men interrogated on television before. I remembered once a man who used to own a clothing factory in Tripoli. He was accused of being a bourgeois and a traitor. He was dressed in a light gray Italian suit that shimmered slightly under the spotlight. He sat stiff in his chair, as if he was in pain. I was standing just outside the entrance of the room, where I wouldn't be seen. Baba and Moosa sat on the sofa, Mama beside them in the armchair. Moosa said softly to Baba, "They deliberately spare the face. I bet his body is a patchwork of bruises." Then a dark cloud grew out of nowhere on the man's groin, a stain that kept spreading. I saw it first. I ran to the screen, stabbing my finger at it. "Move," Baba yelled. I ran and stood beside Mama. "Go to your room," he said. "It's all right," Mama told him and he shouted, "He shouldn't see this." "It's his country too," she said calmly, facing the screen. He stormed out of the room.

We watched the man trying to cover the wet patch with his hands, squirming in his chair.

But to see Ustath Rashid arrested was different. I had heard it said many times before that no one is ever beyond their reach, but to see them, to see how it can happen, how quickly, how there's no space to argue, to say no, made my belly swim. Afterward, when Mama saw my face, she said, "You look like you've seen a ghost." When I told her what I had seen she brought her hand to her forehead and whispered, "Poor Salma." She took me to the bathroom and washed my face. "You shouldn't have watched. Next time run straight home." Then she made me soup and tea as if I had the flu.

★

Somebody, a traitor, was printing leaflets criticizing the Guide and his Revolutionary Committees. They came in the middle of the night and placed them like newspapers on our doorsteps. I say somebody, but there must have been hundreds, maybe even thousands of men. The boys and I took turns staying up, hoping to catch sight of one. We imagined them to be all in black, masked and very fast. Ali claimed he saw one. Masoud whacked him across the head and said, "If you lie about such things again I'll tell Baba."

Everyone feared these leaflets and made a point of tearing them up in full view of their neighbors. Others, like Mama, took them inside only to watch them burn in the kitchen sink, then ran cold water over the ashes. I overheard her once say to Auntie Salma, "They are going to get us all in trouble." When I asked her what she meant, she sighed and said, "Nothing." Another time she stood stiffly out on the pavement listening to Um Masoud speak against the "traitors," saying, "Jafer is very distressed by these leaflets." Mama spoke differently to Um Masoud; she seemed sympathetic. She frowned and shook her head and agreed with everything Um Masoud said. "May God forgive them, they don't know how wonderful the revolution has been for this country."

The morning before Ustath Rashid was taken the boys and I were so bored we took the leaflets the traitors had left during the night and tossed them over the garden walls, where they immediately became, officially, inside people's houses. We only did this in neighboring streets, where we didn't know anyone. We tied their light paper bodies to small stones and hurled them over the high walls the way grenades were thrown in war films. The act was exhilarating, but soon boredom set in again, so we returned to our street and began preparing it for a football match.

Gergarish was a newly constructed district and apart from the main roads that connected it to the center of the city, most of its streets were yet to be named or tarmacked. We called ours Mulberry because there used to be an orchard of mulberry trees here, the last one remaining was next door in Ustath Rashid and Auntie Salma's garden.

The sun reached the center of the sky. We heard the crackle of the local mosque speaker. We could see the pencil-like minaret rise in the distance above the low houses of our street. Then Sheikh Mustafa's voice came.

We marked the goalposts with rocks and empty plastic bottles, argued about the sides and finally the game kicked off. After a few minutes a car hurtled toward us, billowing dust as if it was the only creature in the world. When we saw it, white in the sun, we stopped playing and ran to the pavement, letting the ball roll away.

The car pulled over in front of Kareem's house. Kareem froze, as if his heart had dropped into his shoes. Four men got out, leaving the doors open. The car was like a giant dead moth in the sun. Three of the men ran inside the house, the fourth, who was the driver and seemed to be their leader, waited on the pavement. He smiled at the two fat brothers Masoud and Ali. I didn't register then that he knew them. None of us had seen him before. He had a horrible face, pockmarked like pumice stone. His men reappeared, holding Ustath Rashid between them. He didn't struggle. Auntie Salma trailed behind as if an invisible string connected her to her husband. The man with the pockmarked face slapped Ustath Rashid, suddenly and ferociously. It sounded like fabric tearing, it stopped Auntie Salma. Another one kicked Ustath Rashid in the behind. He anticipated it because he jerked forward just before it came. The force of it made him jump, but he didn't make a sound. He wore that strange embarrassed smile of his. He didn't argue or beg, as if the reasons why, all the questions and answers, were known. His shirt was torn. But no blood. I was surprised by this, and later thought that if he had bled—even a little—it would have made it easier on Kareem, because we all would have respected a bleeding man. Ustath Rashid looked toward us, and when his eyes met Kareem's, his face changed. He looked like he was about to cry or vomit. Then he doubled over and began to cough. The men seemed not to know what to do. They looked at one another, then at Auntie Salma, who had one hand over her mouth, the other clasped around her braided hair that fell as thick as an anchor line over her shoulder. They grabbed Ustath Rashid, threw him into the car, slammed the doors shut and sped between us, crushing our goalposts. I couldn't see Ustath Rashid's head between the two men sitting on either side of him in the backseat; he must have been coughing still.

Kareem took a few steps after the car. For a moment I thought he was going to run after it. He stood with his back to us, then turned and walked home. Auntie Salma was standing, still clutching her hair, looking in the direction the white car had vanished, as if it was arriving, as if Ustath Rashid was in fact finally coming home from a long trip.

★

No one knew why Ustath Rashid had been taken, but the next day the rumors began to spread that he had been a traitor. Um Masoud came to our door, clicked her tongue, looked around her and said, "That's the fate of all traitors."

Baba had heard Um Masoud gossip before: she claimed that Bahloul the beggar was richer than all of us put together, that Majdi the baker didn't only sell "innocent bread"—that was how she put it—but something else too, called grappa, which wasn't only haram, but also illegal in our country. Such rumors didn't bother Baba, in fact sometimes they amused him, but Ustath Rashid was his friend. The two would often go walking by the sea when the sun was low. And many times they sat talking softly in Baba's study, where they were sometimes joined by Nasser. I would bring them coffee. Mama would knock twice, then open the door for me. Walking in slowly, balancing the tray, I would be hit immediately by the coarse, smoke-filled air. It made the bitter smell of cardamom and gum arabic rising up from the coffee almost pleasant. "Don't spill," were often Mama's last words before she swung the door open on those secret meetings. I quickly learned that the best way was to look ahead; not caring if I spilled, or not caring overtly, seemed to be the trick. But at the beginning I walked with my head down, facing the three black pools of coffee on the silver tray, telling my hands to be firm as I caught to my left, in the periphery of my vision, the knees of the two men sitting in the comfortable butterfly-cloaked armchairs, and to my right the brown wooden expanse of Baba's desk. When I had safely placed the tray on the desk, Baba would say, "Well done, Suleiman." When I looked up to face him I sometimes heard my neck crack. Their conversation was suspended from the moment Mama had knocked on the door, they were eager for me to leave. "Close the door," Baba would say, but then he often called me back at the last minute. "Here," he would say, "empty this," handing me an ashtray full of cigarette butts and dead matchsticks. And a few weeks before Ustath Rashid was taken, I placed the tray on Baba's desk and saw tears in his eyes. He was reading something. Ustath Rashid and Nasser were sitting in silence watching him. I went to his side. I nudged him and asked, "Who upset you, Baba?" Ustath Rashid held his hand up and smiled. "I am afraid it's me, Suleiman." I was confused; why would Ustath Rashid upset Baba? Nasser chuckled. Baba put his hand on my head and in a scratched voice said, "No one upset me, Slooma. I was just reading . . ." He looked at the piece of paper in his hand. "It's so beautiful. We will have to publish this," he said, handing the piece of paper to Nasser. Nasser folded it twice and put it in his shirt pocket.

I had never seen Baba cry before. I couldn't understand why reading something beautiful made him cry.

When Baba heard Um Masoud click her tongue and say, "That's the fate of all traitors," he couldn't keep silent. "That's a lie," he told her, his voice bubbling with anger. "A lie the authorities spread to justify the disappearance of the innocent."

Um Masoud studied her fingers, comparing the length of her nails.

"But then they don't need to, obviously; there is always a volunteer more than willing to lie for them. The effortlessness, the automatism by which it happens . . ." Mama tugged at his sleeve. "Let me," he snapped. He squinted his eyes at Um Masoud. "Weeds!" As he spoke the word, he turned his hand as if tightening a screw, as if that word was meant to fix Um Masoud in her corner. "Weeds, like rumors, need no help." Baba's face reddened. It frightened me to see him like this because, although he was often serious, he very rarely became angry.

Um Masoud continued to study her fingers, smiling knowingly now, as if some old suspicion had finally been confirmed.

★

Ustath Rashid had once told Baba that their wives were like two lost sisters who had finally found each other. The first time they met—standing in Auntie Salma's kitchen among the half-unpacked boxes—the two women seemed happy that fate had finally brought them together. Since then, no two days would pass before one called or visited the other. They found excuses to interrupt each other's life. Many mornings Auntie Salma would come to our door to borrow sugar or flour or salt, and Mama would always ask her in. "I am short of time," Auntie Salma would say, but then forget herself until Ustath Rashid or Kareem would come for her, upset she hadn't even started preparing lunch yet. And sometimes it was Mama who went next door, and we were the ones left without lunch. Mama never forgot herself as she did with Auntie Salma.

They drank tea and talked endlessly; occasionally they would hunch over into whispers, then one of them would clap her hands and burst out laughing. They brought the latest music to play for each other, and sometimes one would play the tabla, calling out *aywa aywa* with the beat while the other danced, knocking her hips from side to side. And once I saw them dancing in Mama's bedroom to Julio Iglesias, dancing slowly the way men and women did in foreign films, then Auntie Salma bowed and kissed Mama's hand. Mama pulled her hand quickly away when she saw me. Auntie Salma came to me, held my hands and we danced. She was so sweet, full of smiles, her cheeks red.

When Baba was away and Mama became ill, we didn't answer the door, pretended we weren't in. But once I was so frightened I opened the door for Auntie Salma. She saw Mama on the floor in the bedroom, smelled her. It was as if a black shadow had fallen on Auntie Salma's face. She left the room, then came back with a wet towel. She patted Mama's face. Mama woke up, she seemed disoriented. "What are you doing here?" she said. Auntie Salma helped her up to bed, then asked me to fetch a glass of water. When I returned I found Mama crying. Auntie Salma said, "Praise the Prophet, girl," and with a deep sigh Mama praised.

After Ustath Rashid was taken Mama didn't go to Auntie Salma and Auntie Salma didn't call or visit. Mama didn't want me to see Kareem either. "No need for you to be so close to that boy," she said. She had never called him "that boy" before. "This is a time for walking beside the wall," she said. When I asked her what she meant, she said, "Nothing, just try not to be so close to him, that's all." She could feel my eyes following her, trying to understand, so she added, "It just isn't good for you to be so close to all of his sadness. Grief loves the hollow; all it wants is to hear its own echo. Be careful."

I was affected by Mama's words; I did feel myself nudged by guilt whenever Kareem and I were alone. She was right: a certain sadness had entered his eyes the day Ustath Rashid was taken, but it wasn't the sadness of longing, it was the sadness of betrayal, the silent sadness that comes from being let down. Or at least that's how it seems now. He became quieter—he was always quiet, but not this quiet—and refused to join in any of the games we played. Instead, he would lean on a car nearby as we played football in the street, looking at us in a way that made me feel far away from him. At those moments I wished the Revolutionary Committee would return and this time take my father so that we would be equal, united again by that mysterious bond of blood that had up to that day felt like an advantage.

Later, when we were alone, I told him, "Sorry, Kareem. Sorry we didn't all stand arm in arm to block the way. After all, Mulberry is *our* street." He curled his lower lip and shrugged his shoulders. I felt the way Mama must have felt when, after she had been ill, I was angry at her; I wanted so much to bring him out of his silence. I took him swimming. But instead of heading for the deep, clear waters of the sea that touch the horizon, quickly past the blue-black strip that always frightened us because its floor was alive with dark weeds and movement and things, Kareem swam reluctantly. When I was past the dark waters, moving like a streamer with my long flippers, stabbing my arms fast into the pale turquoise, I looked back and saw him on the shore, walking away.

4

When Baba arrived home the following day he seemed pre-
occupied. It was eight days since Ustath Rashid had been
taken. He didn't bring gifts as he usually did when he returned from his travels. This confirmed that he had been lying: telling us he was going abroad when he was escaping to
his other life here in Tripoli, on Martyrs' Square.

I waited and waited, then asked, "What did you bring me?"

"Nothing," he said without even looking in my direction.

The time before he had brought me a watch that worked
underwater and had its own light. He usually got Mama a
perfume bottle. She would open it, put a drop on the inside
of her wrist, smell it, then smile to herself.

And he wasn't full of stories, nor did he comment about
the things Mama had done to welcome him. She had spent the
whole morning in the kitchen. She hollowed zucchini then
stuffed them with rice and meat. The whole kitchen was alive

with the smell of parsley, lemon and cardamom. She soaked pomegranate seeds in rose water and sugar. Then after she had showered, blow-dried her hair and put on a fresh dress, she burned musk incense sticks and dug them into the plant pots around the house in anticipation of his arrival. She looked beautiful; she always looked beautiful when he was home.

Baba's signature ring was made of one ring followed by three rapid ones: Ding-dong. Ding-dong-ding-dong-ding-dong. Like a rabbit hopping once, then leaping three times. When Mama heard it she picked a pink rose from the vase that was stuffed full of them and planted it in her hair, just above her ear, before running to open the door.

He came around lunchtime, like he said he would. When we sat down to eat he didn't sigh deeply with contentment or say, "There's no place like home." I wished he would because these words always made Mama's cheeks blush. Instead, he stuffed his napkin above the knot of his necktie, stretching his chin toward the ceiling, which made his lips frown, and began sipping his soup.

Mama did all the talking and hardly ate anything. She tried to serve him seconds, but he held his hand over his plate and shook his head.

"Any news of Rashid?"

"We still don't know where he is."

"Faraj, I am worried, worried for us."

"We'll be fine. How's Salma?"

Mama sighed.

"She needs us now more than ever," he said, placed his napkin on the table and left the room.

"You have chosen a dead-end road," she said after him. When he didn't respond she looked at me.

I extended my plate to her, to serve me some more even though I was full.

When he came out of the bathroom he went into the sitting room and shouted, "Where's the tea?" Baba had to have green tea after lunch. He said it aided digestion. It was so bitter it made the roof of my mouth itch.

Now that he was safely in the sitting room and she making tea in the kitchen, I took the opportunity to sneak into their bedroom. I searched his jacket for those huge sunglasses. His scent—a mix of pipe smoke and cologne—felt like a presence in the room. I didn't find them. I went to sit beside him, kiss his hand and tell him how happy I was that he was home, but I found Mama in his arms, her makeup melting. "Come, you know how I hate tears," he told her. She looked at him, attempted a smile. "I need you," he whispered and she nodded wearily. She dried her face and left the room. "Maestro," he said when he saw me. "My darling boy." He got hold of both of my cheeks, pulled me toward him and kissed me on the nose. My cheeks were in agony, tears in my eyes, but I was grinning so broadly I couldn't hide my teeth even if I had wanted to.

Mama returned with the tea tray. Baba nudged me with his knee. I poured the tea, the steam pungent with mint and sage. I held the pot as high as I could, creating as much froth as possible. "OK, enough," he said, but I kept going higher. "Careful," he said anxiously, but I could feel him smiling proudly at me. It made my chest tickle.

When he finished his tea he looked at his watch, stood up and said, "Wake me up at four. I have an important appointment."

"With who?" Mama asked, following him. "But you just got here."

I could hear them talking before they both fell asleep. And although they never woke up before their time, I walked around the house quietly. I listened to the radio low against my ear, sat a few centimeters away from the television. I felt such relief now that Baba was home. Now everything can be normal again, I thought. Now I can leave the house without worrying.

★

Particularly in summer, when the sun swelled with heat, the whole world went to sleep: children, adults, even dogs found a patch of shade to slumber in. I never learned how to nap. It always felt strange to get into my pajamas at three in the afternoon. It reminded me of being ill. Instead I would search the neighboring building plots for things I liked or thought useful, things that used to be knives or parts of old radios, and took them to our garden. There I scraped glue that was always oozing out of the joints of the glue tree, got whatever wood I could find, and carrying everything in the wrap of my arms I climbed the straight flight of stairs up to the flat roof.

The roof tiles were baking, you could see the heat rippling above them. I had forgotten my sandals so I hopped, running for the shadow made by the water tank, to my workshop. I rubbed my feet on the coolness of the shaded tiles. I looked up at the sun. I thought, how strong the sun is, how mighty, and felt frightened by it, by the possibility of it not moving, or coming closer, pressing down against us like a giant balloon. I remembered my Koran teacher Sheikh Mustafa's story of the Bridge to Paradise, the bridge that crosses Hell Eternal to deliver the faithful to Paradise. We all will have to cross it someday, and some of us won't make it.

Those will fall into the fires below, the fires that call for them. What a sight it will be! The heat, the screaming—there's bound to be screaming—the flames licking the sides of the bridge, making the handrails—Sheikh Mustafa said nothing of handrails, but there's bound to be handrails—hot to the touch. "The heat will reach some of us faster than others," Sheikh Mustafa said, "because for some the heat, the fires of Hell themselves, will be like a voice calling." I suppose it's like when you hear your name and you can't help but turn to the source that spoke it. Some of us will be longing for Hell Eternal—God forbid—the way we long to respond, to obey, when our name is called even by someone we have never met before, or by a teacher who has asked a question we know we can't answer: we raise our hand and say, "Yes," and if he can't see us, we reach higher and shout, "Over here, sir!" when we know there'll be nothing to do except curl our lip and shrug our shoulders. Because the fire calls for the fire. Sheikh Mustafa warned me about this; he said, "You must try to ignore the heat, Suleiman. When you are on the Bridge to Paradise, you must keep your eyes focused on Paradise and the beauty of Paradise. And whatever you do, don't look down."

Watching the heat ripple off the tiles on the roof, I thought I should train myself for that day. I decided to walk—not hop, not run, but walk—in a line as straight as an arrow, without even arching the soles of my feet, back to the staircase. The staircase was to be my paradise. The first step didn't feel as bad as I expected, but after a few steps the soles of my feet were on fire and I found myself hopping and running, wondering if hopping and running were allowed on the Bridge to Paradise.

I wished I was like the sheikh. Surely he won't feel any

heat, I thought; the man is holy. He led the prayers at the local mosque. Baba liked his voice, and so after Friday prayer,
later in the afternoon, he had him come to recite some suras
to bless our house. His voice, soaring and expansive, seemed
to reach and fill each room. He was blind. I never got a good
look at his eyes; they were always hidden behind thick black
lenses, but sometimes I glimpsed one from the side, open
and searching for light like a snail waking up in the rain. I
liked to sit beside him, to watch his body flex in a breathless,
suspended moment: his face tilted upward and his right
hand beside his ear, before it comes, his voice, from wherever it comes, and sails throughout our house like a thing
unbound. Sometimes it brought tears to my eyes that I
wiped away quickly. Sometimes I wanted to ask what he
saw, how he imagined us and the world, but I didn't know
how to ask such questions then.

My feet were burning. I ran down the staircase to the
garden and walked under the shade of the small fruit trees,
digging my toes into the cool earth then flicking my feet
ahead with every step, imitating Baba's walk. I picked a blue
plum, but it tasted sour, so I threw it under its tree. Where it
lay I could see my teeth marks and the white gap my bite
had left. At the foot of the wall that separated our house
from Ustath Rashid's house a few mulberries had fallen in
the dirt and were being attacked by ants. This was the last
surviving tree from the mulberry orchard that our street had
erased. I looked up at its thin branches and the small berries
that still clung to them, hanging over the wall. How much
longer before they too will fall to the ants, I wondered.

I fetched the ladder and climbed very slowly. Each berry
was like a crown of tiny purple balls. They reminded me of
the grapes carved into the arches of Lepcis. I decided that

mulberries were the best fruit God had created and I began to imagine young lively angels conspiring to plant a crop in the earth's soil after they heard that Adam, peace and blessings be upon him, and Eve, peace and blessings be upon her, were being sent down here to earth as punishment. God knew of course, he's the All Knowing, but He liked the idea and so let the angels carry out their plan. I plucked one off and it almost melted in my fingers. I threw it in my mouth and it dissolved, its small balls exploding like fireworks. I ate another and another.

I don't know how long I was up on the ladder, but the nearby branches had certainly begun to look barer when I started to feel dizzy. I touched the top of my head, and it was as hot as a car's hood at midday.

The mulberries were so ripe I could see now that many more had fallen on the other side of the wall. Armies of ants, I thought, were probably gathering to eat them. I looked up at the clear blue of the sky and thanked the angels and asked God to please forgive their mischief. I was full, and my stomach wasn't feeling good—this fruit was delicious in the mouth but turned as thick as blood in the stomach—but every time I tried to stop my mouth wanted more. So I decided I would sit over the wall, dangle my feet one on either side as if sitting on a horse and eat all the berries I could reach. I turned and pulled the branches closer. And when I couldn't eat any more I filled my pockets with them.

When I reached the ground I almost lost my balance. I turned on the garden tap and put my head under it. The cold water felt good, but when I stood up I saw the world spin. I quickly put my head under the water again and shut my eyes but saw colors and strange figures dancing. My eyes, shut or open, were covered in a curtain that blurred everything. My ears too filled with a whistling noise. The world turned even faster. I sat where I stood. I felt the damp earth come through my shorts. I must turn off the tap, I thought. Then I heard Mama calling. I pulled out all the berries in my pockets and stuffed them in my mouth, chewing and swallowing as fast as I could. Then I noticed Bahloul the beggar standing outside the garden fence. He was staring at me. How long had he been standing there, I wondered. He pointed his finger at me. "I see you, I see you," he shouted. Although I knew Bahloul was mad, these words, these meaningless words that he always repeated, increased my confusion. I wondered if he thought I was stealing my neighbors' berries and was announcing himself the witness. Was I stealing? I wasn't sure, but I was sure that even if I was I would be forgiven. After all, the berries belonged to Kareem and Ustath Rashid and Auntie Salma. But all that wouldn't matter; if Bahloul went spreading rumors, someone will believe him, because "there's no smoke without fire." My heart shuddered. I tried to look, to seem, to feel innocent because, as Sheikh Mustafa had told me, the innocent have no cause to fear. Mama called again. I leaned against the wall for guidance, hearing the water beat into the dirt behind me. I thought of going back to turn the tap off, but continued walking toward the kitchen. "There's no smoke without fire"; the sentence repeated itself once more in my head.

The cool shade of our house made the blood in my head disappear. Even though I could barely see anything except the movement of this strange curtain of light and dust, I sat down where I knew a chair was. In the distance—could Mama hear him too?—I caught Bahloul screaming fervently, "I see you!" and I wondered if by walking away like that, weak and dizzy, I had confirmed my guilt and so hardened his conviction.

"Why are you wet? What is this red on your hands and face? What is the matter with you? What happened? What happened? And why, in the name of God, why aren't you answering me?"

I sat arched over the kitchen table, my lower lip dripping with saliva. I wanted to speak to comfort her, but I couldn't. My eyes stared into nothing, through a curtain of flickering light. I didn't know what was the matter with me, but was now more concerned for her. Normally, at this time, I would be pulling her hand up the stairs to my workshop to show her what I had made. She would kiss me, then walk to the edge of the roof to look out onto the sea, her long silk house robe, decorated by a giant fanning tail of a peacock, billowing behind her. The sun would be weak and many colors by that time, mirroring itself on the sea. I would stand beside her, leaning against her leg, and every time I looked up her eyes would be fixed and squinting at the shimmering water. She would tell me how the sea changed because the sea changes every day. At those moments I could ask her any question, and she would give me the answer, any question I could think of and as many as I could think of.

"What happened to you?" She banged the table and stood up. I could feel her moving all around me. She began to speak to herself: "It's all your fault. If anything happens to him everyone will blame you, say you were napping while your own son needed you. He's only a child, Najwa, what were you thinking?"

It's very odd to hear your mother call herself by her name, it's very odd to hear anyone do that, but particularly

Mama, because almost no one called her Najwa. To me she was Mama, to her family she was Naoma, and to the rest of the world she was Um Suleiman. Baba called her Um Suleiman or Naoma or Mama and only very occasionally Najwa. It came so sweetly from his mouth.

As I thought this I heard Mama's voice travel and scream Baba's name. I didn't feel myself rise or leave the kitchen but found myself at the entrance of their bedroom. I could barely see her bent over and shaking him. He woke up startled and confused. I wondered if it was four yet, time for his important appointment. They both looked at me. The curtain on my eyes thickened. I saw in Baba's face a look of annoyance at Mama for waking him up like that because there I was standing and obviously all right. Then everything went dark.

5

When I woke up it was night. I felt disoriented. I could hear voices outside but couldn't locate where they were. There was a front half and a back half to our house, divided by the hallway swing doors. In the front there were the formal rooms: the reception room where we received guests we didn't know very well and where I practiced my piano, and opposite the hallway the dining room we never used. In the back there was the sitting room, where we kept the television, then the kitchen, and beyond them the bathroom and bedrooms.

My door was open, and through it I could see that the sitting-room light was on. Mama coughed and asked a question: "Where is he?"

"I don't know. He's lying low until we see what happens to Rashid."

That was Moosa. I loved it when Moosa was here.

"He didn't tell you where he is?"

"No. I have just come from Martyrs' Square, and he wasn't there."

"I told him not to get involved with Rashid and his leaflets."

"Don't worry. Rashid won't talk."

"I am not a child. I know what these people are capable of."

"I drove past the university. The students have taken over the entire campus, hanging banners from windows: *We are not against the revolution, we are against the extremes of the revolution. Autonomy for the student union.* Slogans inspired by *our* leaflets."

I imagined Mama waving her hand beside her ear as she often did when she was hearing something she didn't agree with, because Moosa added, "Um Suleiman, don't be so cynical. These are exciting times. Everything can change."

"Clouds," she said. "Only clouds. They gather then flit away. What are you people thinking: a few students colonizing the university will make a military dictatorship roll over? For God's sake, if it was that easy I would have done it myself. You saw what happened three years ago when those students dared to speak. They hanged them by their necks. And now we are condemned to witness the whole thing again. The foolish dreamers! And it's foolish and irresponsible to encourage them."

"It's our obligation to call injustice by its name."

"Go call it by its name in your country. Here it's either silence or exile, walk by the wall or leave. Go be a hero elsewhere."

"Until when? How long must we bow our heads?"

"Until God rescues us. Nothing lasts forever."

I walked out of my bedroom and heard Moosa sigh.

"Indeed, God never forgets the faithful." He saw me first and began clapping. "O Champion! Welcome, welcome."

Mama rose from the sofa. "How are you feeling? Are you all right?"

"Yes," I said because I knew she needed a quick answer, a quick good answer. I told her I felt good, that I had had the most restful sleep and the most beautiful dreams, and when I said that, the part about the dreams, she asked me to sit down and tell her them.

Mama liked dreams and believed that in them lay secret messages foretelling the future or revealing the true nature of a person. She could tell you what a dream meant because every detail in a dream is a symbol. It's true. For example, a sea in a dream means life. If it's wild and raging you are going to have some hard times, but if it's calm your days will be calm and beautiful. Fish is greed. A girl is good luck and also means life. A boy is very bad luck. But the most important thing to remember about the meaning of dreams is how you feel when you wake up from them. If you have dreamed of a beautiful girl in white drowning in a raging sea and then you were surrounded by a gang of boys beating you with dead fish but you woke up happy, don't worry, don't be afraid, it's a good dream.

I quickly made up a dream where I was walking by a calm sea. Mama smiled and said it was a good omen.

"What else did you dream?" she said.

I thought quickly, but Moosa saved me. He stood up and put me on his shoulders.

Moosa was so tall he had to bow slightly to pass through a doorway. From his shoulders I could see the chandelier's crystals twinkle beside me as he began digging his fingers into my legs. "He's well, he's well," he said. "There's nothing wrong with him. He's the Champion, our big Champion, and there's nothing wrong with him at all. Just look at him, look at his muscles. He's fine, just fine. We all just love to make a big fuss about our Champ."

I had always loved Moosa's massages, but now my body was still stiff from sleep, and it hurt to have him dig his big fingers into my thighs and feet. I giggled.

"I am never invited to lunch parties anymore," Mama said. "And if I invite my friends, they won't come."

"Cowards," Moosa said.

"No, just sensible."

I ran my fingers through the crystal beads of the chandelier. My hands were still red from the mulberries. They looked like a girl's palms hennaed for Eid.

"When was the last time my relatives visited, or his for that matter? And all for what?"

"You can't give people braver hearts."

"No. Only you and my husband and Nasser and Rashid and the naive students you are dragging with you are the brave ones left in this country." She sighed. "Help me," she said, her voice softening. "Help me convince him to leave this wretched path."

"I am not the best person to do that," he said.

"But he listens to you."

Moosa let go of one of my ankles and looked at his watch. The time was nine-ten.

"Who are the faithful?" I asked.

"Put him down," Mama said, and like a crane Moosa arched over. She pressed her hand on my forehead, her skin cool and moist.

"How do you become one of the faithful? I bet their feet won't burn on the Bridge to Paradise."

"He's still warm, but no fever. I will make us something to eat," she said and left the room.

"Food, food, food; when we don't know what else to do, we eat," Moosa said and laughed. Moosa's laugh made you laugh even if you didn't find what he was laughing about funny.

"The boy needs his strength," she said from the kitchen.

He looked at me and smiled. I sat beside him on the sofa, on top of my hands. It was normal for me to do this because my hands were often as cold as "ice cubes." That's what Mama called them. My feet too were often that cold. Whenever they touched hers she flinched, rubbed them or went to fetch a pair of thick winter socks.

"Did you like Lepcis?"

"Yes."

"What did you like about it?"

"The sea monsters. When will you take me to the circus? You promised."

"Maybe tomorrow."

"How do you become a faithful?"

"You pray that the devil won't find you."

"Why is the devil looking for us?"

"It's his job."

"I think mulberries are from Heaven."

I was hoping he would take me into Baba's study and look up some fat book, and we would learn all there is to learn about mulberries.

When Moosa read, you had to stop and listen; he wouldn't have it any other way. He would sit on the edge of his seat and put me opposite him. His hands would change with the words, sometimes quick and urgent and sometimes gentle and slow, and when he would reach a place he liked, he would leave the book open on his lap, clap his hands and sing into the air above us, "Allah! Praise be to Allah how sweet words can be," or about the author, "What's all of this light, this wonder, this spectacular majesty, this precision—absolute precision of language, I swear!" Then he would pick up the book and continue reading.

If it was poetry, he would hold the book with one hand and with the other join index finger to thumb and speak—each—word—as—if—it—was—a—building—standing—alone, and when he found something he liked, he didn't clap or shout praise for the author or the author's family—no—he would pick up his smoking cigarette and take a deep, slow drag while his eyes reread the lines, his leg rocking nervously, then say, with his eyes still on the page, "Do you hear it, Suleiman, the action? The action is always in the words." Then he would repeat the poem and ask me to notice the action this time because poetry, he used to always repeat, is words in action. I tried to understand this when he read from his favorite poet: his compatriot Salah Abd al-Sabur:

> The sky reflects the earth;
> the windows of the sick the bridge lights;
> the eyes of the gendarme the blinking minarets.

I wasn't surprised when I didn't understand such passages. But I was unsettled whenever I recognized something familiar in a poem, something I thought I had experienced:

> Noon, you fill my heart
> with fear and dread, showing
> me more than I want to see.

Or:

Now dusk, now a parting glance,
from the sun leaning fatigued against the hills.
Now, blackness.

And sometimes what unsettled me was the fervor in Moosa's
voice when he read lines like:

The precious robes we wear
have been loaned to us by the Sultan
with whom we have a friendship
as deep and vast as an abyss.

Moosa was very fond of Salah Abd al-Sabur, and when,
in 1981, the poet tragically died at the age of fifty, Moosa
wore a black necktie every day for forty days.

Moosa infected me with his love of language. He did annoy me, though, when, reading prose, he skipped big chunks
or added in his own bits. I could tell when he started adding
because his eyes would leave the page and stare at me. If he
wasn't inventing, then where was he getting it from?

"The person who wrote this big fat book, Moosa, didn't
write these words," I would tell him. "He didn't want them
there or else he would have put them in himself. You can't
put words in his mouth!"

He would smile to himself, jiggle his leg, then slap the
book with the back of his hand. "But he's going in circles."

"Just read it as it is on the page," I would plead.

"But he's fumbling all over the place. He crawls to say
what he wants to say. I know what he's getting at, so let me
bring it to you from the end." Then, in a military fashion, he
would say, "Silence! Full attention!" and resume reading as
soon as he was able to erase the smile from his face.

I was hoping now he would take me to Baba's study and read to me about mulberries. But when I told him that mulberries were from Heaven his response wasn't good. He simply said, "They're a small, soft, stoneless fruit like any other fruit."

"No they aren't. They are the angels' gift. They are a heavenly fruit never intended for this earth, but the angels went behind God's back even though they knew He's the All Knowing and they knew He's the All Seeing because they love us. They risked everything, Moosa, everything, to give us a taste of Heaven in this life. I thought you would know this."

He rubbed his big hands together and raised his eyebrows and stared blankly at me. This was how he reacted when I had asked how babies were made. Then he said, "It's an idea."

Mama came in carrying a large tray, which Moosa bounced up and took from her then placed on the floor. The three of us sat around the food in the center of the room and ate. The bread was hot, and when I tore it, steam billowed out in small clouds. The tea felt good going down my throat, warming my chest.

"Now, Suleiman," Mama said, "you must be careful of the sun. It's OK in the garden, under the trees, but on the naked roof it can kill you, habibi."

My mouth was full so I nodded.

Moosa broke a big piece of bread, held it in between three fingers and scooped up a chunk of tuna; he then dipped it in the harissa and, before a drop could fall, threw it all into his mouth. He too nodded at what Mama had said then sipped noisily at his tea. "The sun!" he finally said. "Oh, the sun, my boy, could kill you." His head swayed with his words and his finger, made red by the harissa, pointed toward the sky, and his big eyes stuck on me like two magnets until I could do nothing but look back into them. He suddenly picked up the small plate of olives and offered it to me. I took one. Then the doorbell rang. It was like a small explosion, for a moment it silenced everything.

Mama looked at Moosa. "God willing, it's him," she said, stood up and ran to the door.

"Didn't I tell you, Um Suleiman?" Moosa yelled after her, "God never forgets the faithful."

6

My ears followed Mama. The doorbell rang repeatedly and in senseless spasms. Still, a mild hope flickered in my chest that it might be Baba. I imagined him leaning with one arm against the door, sweating, bleeding beautifully from one eyebrow and panting—exactly like the heroes I saw in films—waiting for the door to open, to fall into the arms of his wife.

"Coming," Mama said, her voice breathless.

I heard the door open, then a stranger's voice. I was sure he wasn't Baba, but still I asked Moosa, "Is that Baba?"

"Shush," he snapped, straining to hear.

"Yes. Yes," Mama said formally. "This is his home. He's not here . . . But I tell you he's not home."

The man seemed to read his words to her now, delivering them as if they were a line of marching tanks on Revolution Day. Moosa was looking up into nothing, the way people do when they are trying to hear something barely audible, something not meant for their ears.

"You are not coming in," Mama shouted.

Moosa stood up. "Don't leave the room," he whispered and left. I felt a cold shiver pass through me.

Now there was a flurry of voices. I could barely hear Mama. A man shouted, "Get out of my way." How many of them were there, hundreds, thousands? Then amid the noise and the shouting I heard Mama's voice. She sounded like a small nervous fish alone in the deep. "I saw you following me yesterday," she said. "Shame on you following a woman and her son like that. Don't you have anything better to do?"

So they were the same men who had followed us yesterday from Martyrs' Square. The same ones who beat Ustath Rashid and made him vanish. "Vanished like a grain of salt in water" was how Auntie Salma put it, when, after running between police stations and Revolutionary Committee offices, she returned slapping one hand over the other and murmuring, "Vanished like a grain of salt in water." Who have they come to take this time, I wondered: Mama, Moosa, me? How can any one of us prove that he or she is not, and never was, a traitor? How can you prove something that hasn't happened? I bit on my lip to keep my teeth from chattering. I remembered Baba's words, what he whispered in my ear every time he left us: "Take care of your mother, you are the man of the house now." I buried my hands in my armpits, trying to stop trembling.

Moosa attempted to speak in a calm tone, trying to pierce through the chaos. I never felt more grateful for him. But then one of the strangers yelled at him. His voice sounded like an old woman's voice, but you knew he was a young man.

"Who are you?" he shouted.

Moosa tried to reply in the same gentle voice.

"Do you know who we are?" the man shouted again. "Do you? Answer me!"

Everyone else was quiet now.

"Before you speak you must know first who you are addressing," the man shouted.

"He doesn't live here," Mama said.

"Write his name down," the stranger ordered one of his men.

I heard Moosa say his own name with such regret, it reminded me of times when I had no other choice but to admit to my teacher, in front of the whole class, that I hadn't done my homework.

"What's your address? Yes, yes. You live there alone? What are their names? Full names. Isn't he the Egyptian judge? You are his son? Are you related to these people? Then you have no business in this. Step aside," he said. Then at the top of his voice he repeated, "I said, step aside."

Then there was confusion. Moosa said something. Mama tried to come in. I heard the door shut and the voices grow louder. Mama's voice was coming closer; she was walking to where I was in the sitting room. "Please," she pleaded. "I told you he's not here."

"Then why are you worried?" said the man with the old woman's voice.

"My son, you'll frighten him."

My eyes were fixed on the entrance to the sitting room, expecting his figure to appear at any moment. Then there he was, the man in the car, whose dark, pockmarked cheek I could have touched. He stood in the doorway, blocking the only way out. I heard Mama say, "That's him." His suspicious eyes fixed on me. I thought of how, if I had to, I could prove that I was her son.

"Where is your father, boy?" he said.

"He doesn't know," Mama told him.

"Shut up," he snapped, still facing me. His authority was so absolute and sudden it seemed instantly acceptable. "I said, where is your father?"

I shook my head, brought my hand to my chest and waved it as if to say, "I don't know what you are talking about" or "It's not me, I swear, it's not me."

He slapped one side of the doorway and went deeper into our house. Mama followed him. After a few seconds I saw him walk by again. At first I didn't believe it: he was holding in one hand, by the neck, Mama's medicine bottle. Mama stood before him, hunched in despair.

"I beg you," she said, "conceal my shame."

"This is not only forbidden by God and tradition, it is also illegal." He seemed to relish the silence that followed. Then he pushed the bottle into her stomach and said, "But I have other, more important matters to attend to," and with that he walked off. "We will search the place," I heard him say. Mama didn't protest.

★

During this time Moosa must have come to know the men because now he was laughing with them. Then I heard him say, "Um Suleiman, tea please."

"Did you search the house?" the Revolutionary Committee man who was looking for Baba asked his men. "We don't have all night."

"No, no, no, we insist," Moosa said as if they were friends. "Have tea first, then you can search the house. Gentlemen, please, this way." I imagined him leading them into the reception room, perhaps opening one of the windows to let in the fresh sea breeze, doing everything he could to make them comfortable.

I was still glued to my place. I was wet beneath my clothes and realized what I had done. The pee felt warm and cold and sticky on my skin. I could detect the sullen smell of mulberries, rotten and heavy. It turned my stomach. I pressed my thighs tighter together. Then I heard Mama in the kitchen preparing things for them to eat with the tea: because "you must always be generous to those in your home."

I went to the hallway swing doors and held one open to hear what Moosa and the men were talking about.

"A cigarette?" Moosa said. "Cigarette? Would you like one? Have a cigarette, please, go on. Have one, I insist."

"It's not my brand," one voice said.

"What's your brand? Rothmans?"

"Yes," the voice answered, then suspiciously asked, "How did you know?"

"Experience," Moosa said and laughed. "These are just as good. In fact, they are even better. Go on."

"Why?" the man asked suspiciously again. "Is it because they are American?"

"No—Rothmans are American too—but because these are stronger."

"They are all bad for you," another voice came in. "I gave them up eighteen months ago and, believe me, they are nothing but a waste of money and health."

"Exactly," Moosa agreed. "That's why these are better; they are stronger and more expensive, and therefore more devastating." He gave them one of his big laughs that seemed to shake the house, but no one joined him. He fell silent, cleared his throat and said, "Welcome, you have honored us."

I returned to the sitting room. After a few minutes Mama called Moosa. I could hear in her voice how she tried to sound normal. But I could also hear in it a tremor, like during the final moments when the heroine, holding on for dear life, attempts to deliver her last words, something straight and simple, to the one person who is reaching for her hand, the one person who, because of the situation, has been suddenly elevated to the closest soul on earth, her heir, the one to carry her precious last words, and an infinite intimacy is born, a trust unbound and unhindered by the possibility of betrayal—there is no time for betrayal—reaching for his hand and knowing he will not succeed in bringing her back on solid ground, but certain he will remain forever faithful to the moment. I felt the desperate need to go to the reception room, to be that one reaching for her hand.

I heard Moosa excuse himself. His keys shook in his pocket as he walked deeper into the house, bringing with him the odors of the gathering, the stink of smoke heavy with sweat and old stale breath, breath like the breath of fasting men.

"Why this?" she snapped in a whisper. "I don't want those rats in my house. And offering them tea . . ."

"They can put him behind the sun. Better try to win them over. Besides, it might distract them from searching the house."

Moosa's keys shook more furiously now as he carried the tray back to the reception. It must have been very heavy, laden with food, like one of those trays King Shahryar dipped into as he lay listening with lazy eyes to a secretly trembling Scheherazade mill finer and finer the thread of her tales to last a thousand and one nights. How did she do it? How did Scheherazade keep her nerve?

Once I caught my uncle Khaled writing, composing a poem in the garden. He sat in a padded wicker chair, one knee over the other, peering into the sky like someone trying to solve a mathematical problem. Writing required a great deal of concentration. How well would he, Uncle Khaled, the "great poet," as Baba called him, write under Shahryar's sword? What would come out? Could he make music, could he sing? Scheherazade did, night after night, unable to look up into a sky or rest in the silence and solitude of her own garden, hearing a wicker chair creak with the comfort of her own weight. She, I am certain now, was one of the bravest people that had ever lived. It's one thing not to fear death, another to sing under its sword.

Moosa insisted the strangers eat. Whenever one of them declined he pressed them harder, raising his voice and, even though he was a bachelor, threatening to divorce his wife if they didn't eat. This happened several times with gaps of quiet save for the ringing of a teaspoon stirring sugar.

I went looking for Mama. She wasn't in the kitchen. She wasn't in her bedroom either. The bathroom door was closed, but a slice of light came from beneath it. "Mama?" I asked. The silence before she answered seemed endless.

"Yes, habibi."

I didn't know what to say, so I asked, "Do you need anything?"

The door opened. Her face wasn't crying. She placed her hand over my forehead again. Her hand was cold.

"Thanks be to God, you are fine. The fever is completely gone."

"I am sorry, Mama," I said, not sure what exactly I was apologizing for. But I was sorry, I felt my throat tighten as I said it.

"You are well, that's what matters, that's all that matters," she said.

Tears blurred my vision. Then we heard the men by the front door.

"But we are here," the man with the old woman's voice said irritably.

"Listen," another one told him. "We came to find Faraj, not search the house."

I heard one yawn then say, "It's getting late."

"We should search the house now," the pockmarked man insisted.

"Come on, don't be so stubborn."

"Tomorrow's another day," another one said benevolently.

Then we heard Moosa close the door, drive home the bolt.

I looked up at Mama. She was soundlessly mouthing words to God.

Moosa came through the hallway swing doors and went straight into the sitting room. He sat down, speaking to himself, reciting verses from the Holy Koran and adding in his own bits. "Concealer, conceal our faults, protect this house and rid it of all evil, keep away from it all who don't wish it well." Then he quickly repeated, "Concealer, conceal our faults. Concealer, conceal our faults." Mama and I watched him. He stood up, walked around the room, adjusting the curtains, opening some windows. He collected the tray of food that we were sitting around before the men interrupted us, and took it to the kitchen. He returned, sat down and lit a cigarette. He dragged on it hard and when he exhaled he made a whistling sound.

"What did they tell you?" Mama asked him.

He sat on the edge of his seat, his eyes fixed on the space between him and the floor. He looked like he was never going to speak again.

"What did they say?" she asked again, raising her voice. He looked at her. "Have you gone deaf?"

He jiggled his leg and exhaled another whistling tunnel of smoke. He brought his finger to his lips and looked quickly in my direction.

"Suleiman," Mama said. "Go and practice your scales."

7

I never asked to play the piano. It was one of those activities imposed upon me, like school, chess and the infinitely recurring, and therefore seemingly pointless, clipping of my toenails and fingernails. All of which, under the general disadvantage of being a boy, I had to carry out with the necessary degree of earnestness. But, walking to the piano, I felt completely exhausted. I wanted to go and wash and change out of my clothes before anyone discovered I had peed myself. But sometimes you are set on a course and, although you see no sense in it, you are still propelled forward toward it.

At the end of the long and dark hallway a light came from the reception room. Smoke hovered at its mouth. I took short steps and stopped to look behind me. When I reached the room, I saw clouds floating in the center; they were alive with bright silver edges, intertwining like snakes. Sitting on the floor in the sitting room, trying to make sense of what I was hearing, I had imagined Moosa opening the windows, but not even the curtains had been drawn. The room was like a smoke-filled box. The men's places were stamped into the soft cushion seats. I counted them: seven plus Moosa. Seven. They couldn't have all fitted into one car. Only one car came for Ustath Rashid, but they sent two for Baba: four in one, and three in the other, with room for one more, reserved for Baba. In front of each a tea glass stood on the coffee table or, where that was beyond comfortable reach, on the floor or balanced precariously on an armrest. All were empty except for one. I went to it. I sat in the man's place. His seat was still warm. This is where the rude one with the old woman's voice must have sat, I imagined. Only he could be stupid enough to refuse Mama's tea. I remembered his face, how close I was to it at the traffic light, the way he pushed Mama's medicine bottle against her stomach. I recalled how he beat Ustath Rashid. I wondered what it would be like to slap a man, to kick him like that in the behind. I held his tea glass. Cooling, the hot milk had created a skin on the surface, at its center the wrinkled form of a flower or a burn. I blew it carefully to one side and gulped the whole thing in one go. Only after I had emptied it did I realize it wasn't sugared. The bitterness ran through me like a wave.

The bread basket was empty save for crumbs and some of the soft inside of the bread, which, from its color and the way it was rolled into small balls, had been used to wipe hands and mouths clean. I had seen men do this before and once tried it, but Baba said it was vulgar and disrespectful to the bread, to God's gift. Olive stones were strewn on the coffee table, some were even thrown in with the remaining olives, dirtying them. Cigarette butts stood leaning on one another in the empty tea glasses like dead crickets.

From where the men were sitting—from where I was now sitting—they would have been able to see the photograph of Baba on the wall. It was the size of a magazine cover and hung alone, too high up. In fact, it was so high you could easily miss it. In it Baba was dressed in a suit, and behind him there was another photograph of trees in sunlight. It was almost believable that he was standing among the trees and in the sunlight. He was smiling and his eyes looked up into the top left-hand corner of the frame. His cheeks looked too red to be natural, his lips too purple. The photographer painted over it to make Baba look more handsome, less dark. For a long time I believed that photograph: that on that day Baba was in fact standing among trees washed in warm sunlight, his face as pale and pink as an Englishman's. And so, when I realized that the whole thing was a trick, I felt cheated and didn't mind at all that it was hung too high where it could easily be forgotten.

Mama was the one who had insisted I take up an instrument. I was given a choice: the oud, the eighty-one-string qanun or the piano. I opted for the piano because it seemed to be the easiest one to play. I was quick to learn, and enjoyed playing for Mama. Sometimes when I came to the end of a piece, Baba would clap from another room, shouting, "Bravo. Encore," and other times he remained silent.

I suddenly noticed a deep painful thumping in my head. I thought I had better start playing or else Mama might worry where I had gone. I lifted the piano lid; it seemed heavier than usual. My eyes felt hot in their sockets. I pressed my cold fingers against them. At this moment Moosa walked in.

"It's so stuffy in here," he said, and opened the windows. He walked across to the dining room on the opposite side of the hallway and opened the windows there too, and only then did the air move. The smoke disappeared and the breeze that came was a night breeze lightened by the sea. Breathing it seemed to wash my insides. The thumping in my head eased.

"Enchant us, maestro," Moosa said, then pulled out the cushion seats and beat them together in pairs as if he was clapping. He stacked the tea glasses on top of one another, placed them on the tray and carried it all to the kitchen. He returned with the vacuum cleaner and began hunting all the scattered bread crumbs.

I found Mama in the kitchen, washing dishes.

"Um Suleiman," Moosa yelled above the hum of the vacuum cleaner, "leave those for tomorrow."

"It's all right," she said softly to herself. "They won't take a minute." She knew he couldn't hear her. Why speak if no one can hear you? I felt my cheeks burn with an anger that seemed to come from nowhere. She tilted her head and mumbled a few more words to herself, words that were impossible to hear, wasted words, like food thrown away, like the ripened mulberries in the dirt, good only for ants, like the bread used to wipe mouths and hands, like the few good olives that were soiled with olive stones that had been scraped with teeth, had tongues curled around them, sucking them dry. Her back shuddered. Mama was crying. I felt my anger doubling. I slapped the table. She jumped, her soapy hand on her chest. "What's the matter?" she said, turned off the running water, and sat beside me. She placed her hand on my knee. "What's the matter, habibi?" she whispered. She held my hand and shook it gently as if to wake me up, to remind me of something, and asked again in a whisper, "What's the matter, habibi, light of my eyes?" She looked older. I longed for how things had been.

We would by now still be sitting on the floor in the sitting room, playing cards, drinking tea. Moosa would take the newspapers and read out loud his favorite articles of the day. Mama would comment and tell him off every time he skipped or added his own words, and I would roll on the floor laughing as they argued. Baba would arrive, take off his tie and shoes and talk to us for a few minutes before going in to shower and pray. He would reappear comfortable in his white jallabia, smelling of French cologne. Moosa would reread the day's articles to him and Baba never minded Moosa's skipping or adding. Baba listened to him in a way that always pleased Moosa, and so he read louder and for longer stretches of time.

Baba never spoke about it, but Moosa had told me how special their friendship was, and when he talked about it you could hear in his voice how much he loved Baba. He looked up to him like an older brother; you could see it in his eyes when they were together.

When Moosa's father, Judge Yaseen, tried to force his eldest son to complete his law degree, Baba stepped in in Moosa's defense. A prominent Egyptian judge who was invited personally by King Idris to help reform Libya's courts, Judge Yaseen wasn't a man who was easily crossed. He was tall and solemn, always dressed formally in jacket and tie even on Fridays. His hair was always slicked back and gave off a weak shine. I had never met anyone like him before. For a long time I believed he knew everything there was to know in the world. It was his reserve, the stubborn cloud of earnestness that seemed to follow him wherever he went, that intimidated me. Later, when I discovered that reserve and earnestness weren't necessarily traits of wisdom, I feared him less and began to see his manner as affected and later still came to forgive him for it and only then did I love him. Because, as fate would have it, Judge Yaseen was to become my guardian. If I had known this as an intimidated child, I might have run away into the sea to escape my fate.

Whenever the judge was present people talked less. He almost never asked a question. His eyes were brown and deeply set and a little too small for his head; when they fixed on you they made your skin itch. Every time we met he would simply declare, "You are well" or, "You will pass your exams," and, when it was time to part, "You will be careful." And although I felt the urge to say, "No I am not well, and no I won't pass my exams or be careful," my head always betrayed me and I would nod. His whole demeanor was hypnotic.

After Qaddafi's September Revolution overthrew King Idris, Judge Yaseen didn't return to Cairo. He opened his own practice in Tripoli and dreamed of the day his eldest son, Moosa, would join it.

Moosa fulfilled all of what was required of him. He accompanied his father to funerals and on formal visits, and when the judge couldn't attend Moosa put on a jacket and tie and bore his father's condolences or compliments. But when he was one year short of completing his law degree—it took him five years to pass the first three—Moosa decided to quit. Judge Yaseen refused even to discuss it.

The judge was Baba's friend and lawyer. They met after a shipment of oak that Baba had purchased "in good faith" never arrived. Out of all the men in the judge's domino circle, Baba was the youngest and the only one who wasn't a judge. They gathered every Thursday afternoon, just when the sun was softening, to play dominoes and enjoy the uninterrupted view of the sea from Judge Yaseen's second-floor balcony. The judge and his family, including Moosa, also lived in Gergarish, but of course the judge didn't call it that; he called it by its other, fancier name that made you think it was a place in Italy, not Tripoli: Gorgi Populi. This is what it was called when Libya was an Italian colony. "We reside in Gorgi Populi," he used to say. Moosa always looked embarrassed.

When I used to cycle by with the boys, happy the school week had ended, I would see the old men and Baba sitting around their dominoes. Baba would ask urgently, "What? Is anything the matter?" leaning over the railing. After I had reassured him, waving at him as if to say, "I don't know what you are talking about" or "It's not me, I swear, it's not me," he would ask me to come up and say hello. The urgency with which he greeted me then whenever we met outside our home makes me wonder now, as I reflect on those distant days, whether he was totally ignorant of his wife's "illness."

I always went to him first and kissed his hand in the way he taught me—I only had to kiss it once in the morning and once at night, but it pleased him when I did it in front of his friends. I preferred to shake hands with the old judges, but there were always one or two who pulled me and kissed me on both cheeks. Because they were old, their lips were soft and wet. It took a lot to stop myself wiping my face in disgust. They always said the same things: "Mashaa Allah. A man now, our young Suleiman. How old is he today? What year at school?" This attention brought a big smile to Baba's face. Then, in a very earnest voice, he would ask,

"What have you been up to, young man?" He only called me "young man" at such occasions. Something about this strange way he spoke made some of the old judges smile, and so I believed he did it to amuse them. "OK, enough playing now," he would finally say, even though I wasn't playing, I had come up on his request to say hello to his friends. "It's time you were home, young man." As soon as I left the balcony I would wipe my cheeks clean. Once, when I was running down the staircase, Baba called me back. I found him standing outside the front door. "What?" I said. He kissed me on the head and gave me ten dinars, the same amount of money I found beneath my pillow on birthday mornings.

Out of all of his father's friends, Moosa picked Baba to convince the judge of his plan to quit university. They met several times in our house, closing the door to Baba's study behind them as if they were planning a revolt, and talked for hours.

Baba convinced the judge to allow Moosa to take a year off by offering to employ him. But before the year ended Moosa was confident that he wasn't going to resume his law degree at Garyounis University, which was in Benghazi, twelve hours' drive from Tripoli. Judge Yaseen was furious when he heard of his son's decision, Baba was responsible, and Moosa was independent.

This history had brought Moosa closer to our family and allowed the judge to blame Baba for every misfortune that Moosa encountered. "You have ruined my son, Bu Suleiman," the judge would loudly let slip to Baba in front of the others during a domino game. "Don't add salt to the wound by beating me in the game I love in my own house." And I once heard Baba tell Mama, "He can't be upset at me forever. At least in his house I am guaranteed his wrath will be limited."

Relations between the three men didn't get easier after all of Moosa's business projects failed. He had a chicken farm, but the chickens got too hot by day, too cold by night and so died one after the other. It was a catastrophe: one thousand chickens in less than one week! But even though he had lost all of his money—which he had borrowed from Baba—Moosa insisted on giving them a proper burial. "Why punish them in life and in death?" were his words. He hired a big yellow tractor with the letters "JCB" written on its sides. He carved a big mass grave for his one thousand dead chickens, buried them, then got me to sit on his lap and drive the tractor several times over the earth. It was a kind of ceremony for his dead chickens. I remember, after we were done, a few feathers that had survived the burial clinging to the yellow metal of the tractor.

Another time he imported tires from Poland. For days all he spoke about was how Polish car tires were destined to be world famous. "Mark my words, as we now know China for silk, Japan for televisions, New Zealand for sheep, Poland too will become known for car tires. You will see, this will be the most successful import into Libya since JCBs."

Well, he imported the Polish tires and, as with the chickens, he didn't order a few to try out first, he bought a whole shipload. "When the market demands, Slooma, you must be in a position to respond," he said, walking me through the warehouse where they were stored. It was strange and wonderful to be surrounded by columns and columns of black rubber tires piled on top of one another. Moosa's lips were moist, and he had a big proud smile on his face.

The tires sold very well, but, as soon as August came, Moosa's Polish tires melted. It was a big problem—and it definitely wasn't funny—because his customers, feeling cheated, returned to him furious, demanding their money back. On one occasion the tires melted completely, gluing the car to the road. In a fit of rage, its owner threatened to teach Moosa a "good lesson." On more than one occasion Baba had to intervene to rescue Moosa from an angry customer. He would pay them back their money, apologizing repeatedly, unable to completely lose his smile. And to the man who wanted to teach Moosa a good lesson, Baba paid more money, apologized harder and, after the man was gone, burst out laughing.

Moosa refused to talk about this venture. The only explanation I ever remember him giving for his mistake was "It doesn't get very hot in Poland." Mama and Baba didn't allow him a grieving period, they immediately started teasing him about the episode: "Moosa, how's the weather in Poland today?" "Listen, do you think we can have another set of those world-famous tires for next winter?" "For God's sake, Moosa, if you marry a Polish girl, remember to take her home during the summer."

And there we could have all been, talking, reading and laughing. Instead Mama was now sitting in front of me at the kitchen table, her eyes like a bird's, dark and full of grief. Moosa was still vacuuming the reception room. And Baba . . . I hadn't seen him since I came in from the garden, when Mama ran and frantically shook him to wake up. "Where's Baba?" I finally said. "Why isn't he home yet? What time is it?"

Mama didn't reply, she seemed to be thinking about my

questions: why I was asking them and what the thoughts were behind them. Then she broke out, "Why are you asking about your father now? What's the matter, am I not good enough for you? Why don't you speak up and explain to *me* what's going on?"

I heard the vacuum cleaner's loud hum fall to nothing. Moosa must have heard her shouting and was now coming to my rescue, I thought.

"I want to know where Baba is. Why isn't he home?" I yelled at her.

Moosa walked in, he tried to say something, but Mama told him to mind his own business. I began to cry.

"Now you listen," she said. "I have enough to deal with here, don't drive me crazy. And . . . And . . . What's this smell?" she said and began searching with her nose. "Piss!"

"No, it can't be," Moosa said.

"I smell piss," she said, her eyes wide open.

I squeezed my thighs together and pressed my mulberry-stained palms on my wet lap. She pulled my hands away, I struggled against her but she was stronger than me. She rubbed the wet fabric of my jallabia and smelled her fingers.

"What's going on with you?" she shouted. She faced Moosa, slapped her own thigh, then pointed at me and said, "He peed himself." She pulled me up on my feet and shouted, "You are no longer a baby. Why didn't you go to the toilet? Talk!"

"Where is Baba?" I cried.

"What were you up to in the garden? Why did you flood the entire place? Why are your hands stained red? Why did you pee yourself?" she said, shaking me with each question, then she fell into her chair and began to cry. "What do you all want from me? Do you want me to lose my mind?" She buried her face in her hands and, not moving, not making a sound, sat like this.

"I am sorry, Mama," I said into the cold silence. "I promise I will never do it again, please don't cry."

A low, strangled sound came muffled through her hands. Her crying was not normal. Mama's ill again, I thought. I looked at Moosa. She began speaking, but I could hardly make out the words, things about her bad luck and how since childhood she had been cursed with bad luck, bad luck bad luck bad luck, calling for her dead Baba to come back and help her, pleading with him to return and save her because it was too soon, she said, all too much and too soon. She wept. Then she spoke to Baba, blaming him for his dreams, his crazy dreams that put the whole world at risk. "Who do you think you are?" she said, as if there was a small version of him standing on the breakfast table in front of her, "Saying, 'We must inspire the young. We must open their eyes to other ways, other possibilities.' Well, there you have gone and opened their eyes all right. Happy now? Now they have been inspired. Inspired to madness, inspired to craziness. What have you done, you crazy fool? What have you done?" she cried, holding her head.

"Praise the Prophet, Um Suleiman, and bid away evil spirits," Moosa said from behind me.

This is a good trick. Whenever someone is very upset or angry, ask them to praise the Prophet and they have to stop yelling or crying and praise.

After a long silence she sighed deeply and said, "Peace and blessings be upon him."

I was still standing beside her, facing her, waiting for something, something she would say or do to make everything different. She looked at me and smiled, but quickly her smile collapsed into a frown. She held her arms out and tilted her head like a girl wanting to hide. She hugged me. I could feel her wet lips on my neck, her breath warm and irregular. "I am sorry, habibi," she mumbled. "You were frightened. Forgive me." I patted her back and whispered what I sometimes said when she was ill, when I had nothing to say but couldn't remain silent: "Everything is going to be fine." She dried her tears, took a deep breath and nodded. "Did you know how hard the angels worked and how they risked everything to give us mulberries?" I said to make her better, to make her cheeks rosy again. "And all because they knew how hard life was going to be for us here on earth. I wish you were there with me, to taste them. You know how you say that everything we know will be more beautiful in Paradise? Well, everything except mulberries, they taste just as good here, they are the angels' way of making us patient. I think they are the only thing here from Paradise. I wish I had saved some for you. Perhaps tomorrow I'll find some more, I'll see." She held my cheeks in her hands and kissed my forehead. "You are my prince. My beautiful prince," she said and smiled.

★

After I had showered and gone to bed, Moosa came in and switched on the light. "How about a rub before you slumber, you prince you," he said, hoping to make me laugh. I said nothing. I was upset at him for doing nothing, for standing there watching it all, and now for switching on the light just when my eyes had become used to the dark. I was lying on my stomach, I didn't even turn to face him. He sat beside me and began digging his big fingers into my shoulders, running them like giant forks up and down my back, sideways too. I heard him sigh with the effort. Apart from that he was silent.

I never liked being upset at Moosa, but I couldn't stop, didn't know how to be normal again, to laugh and play with him. He didn't finish, didn't give me one of his mammoth rubs where every limb, every finger and knuckle was squeezed and twisted and pulled. He quickly kissed the back of my head, switched off the lights and left.

I heard them talk, then the front door shut. Moosa had left. Walking into the night. His car dark and cold, I imagined. I heard the engine not start until the third or fourth time, then gaining speed, leaving us, vanishing into the silence.

8

That night I dreamed of Baba floating on the sea. The water was unsettled, moving as it does in the deep, rising and falling in hills. He lay on his back. He looked like a small fishing boat trying to surrender to the sea. I was there too, working hard to keep my shoulders above water, to not lose sight of him, but the sea rose, and he vanished from view. I kept swimming. I knew I was close. Then I saw him, wooden and stiff. When I reached out to touch him he turned into a fish, agile and shy. He plunged with a splash down and away. I could see his silver spine flicker below the water. I turned around and saw no shore to return to.

When I woke up I found myself in his place, in Mama's bed. I buried my face in his pillow and smelled the salt of his neck. Beneath the pillow my hands met his leather note-book. He always hid it there in case he had a dream. A slim golden pen was fixed on its spine and acted as a lock. I pulled it out and opened the notebook. Baba's handwriting filled the pages from edge to edge and from top to bottom. There was only one blank page left at the end. He could barely record one more dream here. I watched his curling blue writing interrupted only by the straightness of an *alif* or a *laam*, like the lampposts and palm trees that line Tripoli's sea front. His dots were more like small dashes flying in the same direction, like birds or confetti scurrying above the speed of his writing, chasing a dream before it could escape his memory. I recalled his form—many mornings I had seen him like this—sitting in bed, the gentle and modest slope of his bare back hunched over this small book that wasn't longer than his index finger, recording a dream he had just woken from. When he heard me enter the room, he would lift his other arm in the air like a football referee. I locked his book with the golden pen and placed it back beneath his pillow.

Beside me, where Mama had slept, I saw the sheets disturbed, the form of her head in the pillow. There was no reason why, I thought, we shouldn't sleep like this every night, she and I together in her bed. She never spent the night here when Baba was home, and because my bed wasn't wide enough for the two of us she slept alone on the sofa in the sitting room. A good solution, I thought, was to have Baba sleep in my room and, because neither Mama nor I snored, we could have the big bed all to ourselves.

That was the excuse Mama gave for sleeping on the sofa. I never heard him snore. "Of course you never have," she would say. "He only snores when he's very deeply asleep and that only occurs in the middle of the night when you yourself are deeply asleep." I found it hard to believe, particularly that when he snored, Mama said, it was so loud the mattress vibrated. I didn't ask any more questions because I sensed in her voice, in the repetition "you yourself," an irritation that was as much aimed at me as it was at Baba or even at herself.

During those nights, when Baba was home and Mama dragged her blanket behind her to the sofa in the sitting room, I felt something rise like a dark liquid from around our feet, separating us, sending each one sailing alone through their individual night where morning seemed too distant and abstract to be trusted. It wasn't until we were gathered around the breakfast table in the sun-flooded kitchen that I felt it recede.

Lying in bed, I would see the light from the television in the sitting room flicker on the darkened walls outside. From her makeshift bed she would lie late into the night watching Egyptian romance films where lovers and love are never satisfied and where after a single word or glance violins would begin to whine. As I live now in the country that produced those films I am familiar with their shortcomings. Their melodrama seems to mock love. That's how I explain the melancholy I felt then as a boy, lying in my bed until the early hours of the morning, listening to the violins blaze out before Mama quickly turned down the volume. She must have sat on the edge of her seat, ready for the violins, impatient for the moment that would come to strengthen her doubts about love and confirm her instinct to go without it, accepting—always accepting—a life forced upon her.

Some nights she started in her room but in the morning I would find her pillow and blanket in the sitting room, her shape within them, an ashtray beside her full of crumpled tissue paper.

On some winter mornings when the sky remained stubbornly dark, I sneaked into her makeshift bed fully dressed in my school uniform, feeling my tie tug at my neck as I coiled within the cave of her blanket, my cheek warmed by her pillow, wondering how can Heaven be anything other than this?

They—Mama and Baba—only lay together for their afternoon nap, and that was because the curtain in their room was made of thick velvet that kept the sunlight out and, I assumed, the two-hour nap didn't allow enough time for Baba to reach the depths of sleep necessary for snoring.

I always suspected there was a different reason why, when Baba was home, Mama didn't sleep in her room. I don't know why, but something in me blamed her for it. Irritation rose in my throat when I questioned her about his snoring. But this changed when one night I saw them together. Everything inside me changed.

Something seemed to wake me that night and take me to their room. Baba's bedside lamp was the only light on, and under its faint glow I saw him on top of her, moving back and forth the same sad, short distance, like one of those old ladies mourning the dead. I was standing in the dark, at the entrance of their room, where they couldn't see me. She lay beneath him, unmoving, looking away. I couldn't see her face. One of her arms lay stretched beside her, the hand open and slack toward the sky. He moaned a strange moan, stubborn like a saw. Then suddenly he froze, his back stiff and shuddering, before he fell to one side. He lay breathing heavily, staring into the ceiling. I could see his penis sloped to one side, glistening under the light of his bedside lamp. She, too, was naked. Her night dress was rolled up to her armpits. Her breasts quivered oddly when she moved to grab the bed sheet. She pulled it up to her chin, turning away from him. She cleared her throat, said, "Turn off the light, I told you to turn off the light." He put out the lamp and from within the darkness I heard his body move. I wondered if he was coming close to her again.

Had the Great Throne been disturbed, I wondered? I remembered Sheikh Mustafa's words: "Every time a man and a woman lie together outside of wedlock God's own Seat shudders." Baba and Mama weren't like that, they were married on God and His Prophet's Sunna, but something about what I saw disturbed me so deeply that I couldn't imagine how God's Seat, His Great Throne, didn't shudder as my heart did.

I lay that night unable to sleep, wondering—and feeling fear, guilt and anger at my wondering—if I shouldn't have done something to stop it; if unbeknownst to me Mama needed my help. I became certain it was Providence that woke me. Why else, then, was I woken at such an hour? Providence it must have been. And what a failure I proved myself to be. A failure for lacking the courage—or whatever it is that enables people to act quickly, decisively and without doubt—to rise to the occasion, to prove myself one of the faithful. I was called to stop something terrible, something that the angels I was certain never blessed, something that made Mama leave her bed every night to sleep on the sofa alone, fading, as I was fading, into sleep on the ridiculous violins of an Egyptian romance film.

I was lying in their bed thinking all of this when I heard the doorbell ring, then Moosa's voice. From the way he spoke I suspected he was either carrying something heavy, like a new sack of rice, or hot fresh bread from Majdi the baker.

"What do I want with that?" Mama told him.

"It's a camouflage," he said.

"But it's huge!"

"Did you gather all the papers and books I told you about?"

"Yes, everything is ready."

"Are you sure? Bu Suleiman doesn't want us to miss a thing."

When they heard me walk out they stopped talking. After a short silence Mama whispered, "He's up." "Slooma!" Moosa yelled in the exaggerated way football fans do when their star player appears on the field, whistling, making the sound of a crowd's roar, raising his fist above his head.

I went to the bathroom. I heard them resume their conversation, whispering. When I entered the kitchen they fell silent again. He was sitting at the breakfast table, she stood with her back to me, washing fruit.

"How did you sleep, Champ?"

"Good," I said.

"Mama told me you had a bad dream."

"I don't remember," I said.

"Well, it might have been the aftereffects of the sunstroke. The heat probably melted your brain," he said and laughed so loudly even Mama couldn't resist. She covered her mouth with the back of her hand, but she made no sound. She could have been crying for all I knew. She turned and placed a plate of fruit on the table. I looked into her eyes, they weren't crying.

"How did I come to be in your bed?" I asked.

"Good morning, habibi." She kissed me. "You had a bad dream. You don't remember? You were crying."

I shook my head. I remembered the dream I had of Baba in the sea, his silver fish spine beneath the water.

"You lay beside me mumbling and trembling."

I held her hand to kiss it as I did every morning, but the telephone rang, and she went to answer it.

Moosa grabbed an egg, cracked it against his forehead, peeled it, squeezed half a lime on it, rolled its shiny white body on the three small mountains of salt, black pepper, and cumin, then handed it to me. He took to reading the paper out loud, but I was feeling myself become restless, as if I was neglecting something else much more important. This made me unable to concentrate, and it irritated Moosa. He flexed his jaws, jiggled his leg, lit a cigarette and read to himself.

Resting behind him against the kitchen counter was the back of a framed picture. This must have been the heavy object he had carried in. Mama was right, it was huge. She ran back into the kitchen.

"That was them," she said. "I am sure it was them. I could hear a man breathing on the other end. I tried to get him to speak. But he hung up." She was rubbing her palms together. "Come on, let's get on with it before they arrive."

Moosa stared at the table. His jaws flexed rapidly and every time they did two small round pockets inflated below his ears. "Where's the hammer?" he said.

"I don't think we've got a hammer," Mama said, pulling open a few drawers in the kitchen. "Honestly, I don't think we've got one."

"It doesn't matter," he said and took off his shoe. "Just give me a nail."

"I don't think we've got nails either."

"I should've known," he said irritably and with his shoe in his hand limped to the reception room. I followed him. He took down Baba's picture, the one that hung too high up on the wall. He tested the strength of its nail, then whacked it a couple of times with the heel of his shoe. "That should do it," he said to himself and left the room.

Baba's picture stood on the floor, leaning against the piano stool. His smile changed, he looked as if he was embarrassed now, and the trees behind him looked even less lifelike. Moosa returned, hugging the huge frame. On either side of him I could see a man's shoulders. They were decorated with stars and eagles. Moosa was breathing heavily. He nudged the picture up, came down a little, then pushed it up again. "Suleiman," he said hoarsely, and I put my ear against the wall. "Up a little," I said. But he put the picture down. He caught his breath then gripped the frame again. "Down a little," I said. "A bit to the right." We stepped back and watched the Colonel stare up and into the distance. His cap down to his eyes, as if something in the sky bothered him, black tufts of hair gathered around his temples and ears and the sides of his neck, two mysterious lines carved into his cheeks like brackets on either side of his mouth. The brass plaque on the frame read: *Colonel Muammar el-Qaddafi, the Guide of the Libyan Popular Revolution.* "The Benefactor, the Father of the Nation, the Guide!" Moosa said with a smile. He punched the air with his fist, chanting, "El-Fateh, el-Fateh, el-Fateh," pretending to be several thousand people. I didn't laugh. He then hid Baba's picture behind the piano and put on his shoe. When we returned to the kitchen Mama wasn't there. Moosa took his chair by the table and lit a cigarette. I remained standing, watching him. After a little while he yelled, "Um Suleiman, how are you doing?" And under his breath he said, "The bastards." When he saw that I was watching him he smiled weakly. "Why don't you sit down?" I didn't know why I didn't want to sit down, and didn't like feeling the pressure of having to explain myself.

"Come and give me a hand," Mama yelled from her bedroom.

He put out his cigarette and said, "Sit down."

I remained standing. He left the kitchen. He was acting as if suddenly he was the man of the house and I the guest. His broken cigarette burned in the ashtray, I watched it until it died.

Then they both reappeared carrying mountains of books and papers. He held the garden door open for her, she ran out. Before he could follow a book fell. I was about to fetch it for him but hesitated. He looked at me. I saw a shadow of disappointment in his eyes. I wonder now in what way I had disappointed him: was it by not picking up the book, by lacking that thing that enables people to act quickly and without doubt? Was it by not obeying him when he asked me to sit down? Or was it something else, something more intangible than a single act? Disappointment was a series of shadows each pointing to the other. He left the book on the floor and went after Mama. After a moment I picked it up and followed them.

Outside, the morning air was sweet and the birds sang as if they were clearing their throats for the day. When I reached the stairs I saw the peacock on Mama's house robe disappear on to the roof, Moosa following close behind, taking two steps at a time. I climbed at my own pace, occasionally slapping the book against my thigh, rubbing it against the wall. On its spine the word "Democracy" was written, below it the word "Now."

Moosa was on his knees beside the water tank where I had my workshop. He took the tin bucket where I kept my tools and with one motion chucked its contents to one side. He tore a few pieces of paper, then lit and threw a match after them. Dark smoke appeared. He blew at it, and it stopped smoking, and although you couldn't see the flames you knew they were there by the way they made the air around them ripple. I thought of protesting the use of my bucket, but it was too late. Their urgency seemed to cancel everything around them.

Mama quickly shuffled through the papers in her hand, and when the fire was good and strong she began throwing them, one at a time, as if feeding a dog, into the bucket. I watched Baba's writing curl, turn red, gray, then vanish into black ash. I came closer to hand Moosa the book, but caught Mama, from the corner of my eye, looking at me. I feared she would send me away to practice my scales so I held the book behind my back and didn't move. Moosa continued tearing the books. I was surprised by how easily they came apart in his big hands.

Holding the hot tin bucket with his white handkerchief, he took it down to the garden. Mama followed him, saying, "You find a spot, I'll get the spade."

I remained on the roof, holding the book behind my back, looking down at them. He chose the spot I had flooded in the garden by the glue tree. Mama came running, her peacock robe flying behind her, and handed him the spade. I watched him digging and burying the ashes. After they were finished they walked back to the kitchen.

Standing on the roof, I remembered how once, when she had woken from her nap, I brought her up here. She was still lazy with sleep, walking behind me in her long, loose robe. I, too excited to wait, pulled her up the stairs to my workshop to show her what I had made: a horse out of wood, bubble

gum for ears and radio wires coiled together to make the
tail. I made it because the day before she had said, "You are
my prince. One day you'll be a man and take me away on
your white horse." She kissed me, walked to the edge of the
roof to look out on to the sea. The sun was dying, pouring
itself into the water. I stood beside her, leaning against her
leg. When I looked up her eyes were fixed and squinting at
the light. "The sea has changed again," she said. "Every day
the sea changes." Then she was silent. From within my core,
a place mysterious until that moment, I felt I was melting,
that I, too, like the sun emptying itself into the sea, was
pouring myself into her.

I stuffed the book into my shorts, covering it with my
T-shirt, and sneaked into the kitchen. Mama was standing at
the sink. I ran to my room. The moment I closed the door
behind me I heard Moosa leave the bathroom, then the
sound of the cistern filling up. I had just missed him. A sweet
sensation of guilt and excitement ran through me, remind-
ing me of the time I had once stolen a cigarette from him and
lit it beneath my bed. I was seven or maybe even six. When
Mama caught me she slapped me on the back of the hand
three times. I hid the book beneath my pillow and, fearing
my absence would raise suspicion, returned to the kitchen.

I sat at the table, opposite Moosa. When his eyes met
mine he smiled. He grabbed an apple, sliced it and gave me
a piece. I held it between my fingers, feeling its cool moisture
against my sweaty skin.

"Why do the Revolutionary Committee want to search
our house?" I asked.

Moosa's eyes looked past me at Mama.

"You can't keep a thing to yourself," she told him.

He put his hands up as if something was about to fall

from the sky. "I didn't tell him a thing, he saw us burning the books."

"And who brought him to see? Why, Moosa? Why? Can't you keep anything to yourself?"

Seeing how upset Mama had become made me, too, feel angry at Moosa. He wasn't trying to defend himself anymore; he sat, arms folded, facing the table. I placed the slice of apple he had given me on my plate, its flesh already beginning to brown.

"Children aren't suppose to know these things. I wish I hadn't told you, I wish I had never told you anything." Then came the long silence that usually succeeded their arguments.

"Why did you burn Baba's books? Baba loves his books." Neither of them looked at me. "I don't think Baba will be happy that you two burned his books."

"There you go. What are you going to tell him now?" Mama said. "Go on, tell him," she shouted. Moosa stared at the table. "Tell him about his father, your hero." She was beside him now. She nudged him several times, repeating, "Tell him, tell him." For a moment she seemed to hesitate, then she said, "Tell him that you encouraged him, looked up to him to guide you, inflated his chest with your adoration."

Moosa's leg began to jiggle. "Enough," he said.

"Now you say 'enough,' after pushing him and pushing him."

"I never wished him harm."

"It's different for you. You are Egyptian. The most they could do is deport you."

"I would give my life for him."

"You can die ten times over, it would do no good now."

Moosa's lips were red, and a purple shadow covered his cheekbones. He looked as if he had been slapped. I wondered if that was the way he looked when the man from the Revolutionary Committee, the one with the old woman's voice, shouted at him, asking all of those questions about where he lived and who he lived with, questions you would ask a small boy lost in the street.

"You can't blame me for this," he said.

"You are children playing with fire. How many times I told him: 'Walk by the wall, feed your family, stay home, let them alone, look the other way, this is their time not ours, work hard and get us out of here, let me see the clouds above my country, Faraj, I want to look down and see it a distant map, reduced to lines, reduced to an idea. For your son's sake. In five years he'll be fourteen, they'll make a soldier out of him, send him to Chad.' How many times I repeated it! 'Five years!' he would mock. 'In five years everything will be different.' Now look where his recklessness has led us."

"Bu Suleiman is an honorable man who wants a better Libya for you and for Suleiman."

"And who does he think he is to want that!" Mama yelled back. Her voice was strained, it made it impossible to argue with her. "They are mighty. He thinks he alone can beat them?"

"He's not alone."

"Oh, my apology, I forgot about the handful of men with nothing better to do but hide together in a flat on Martyrs' Square and write pamphlets criticizing the regime. Why hasn't anybody thought of that, I wonder? Of course, that was the answer all along; how foolish of me. Look now where it has led you. A massacre is in the making. God knows if Rashid will make it, the poor man, stupid enough to believe your dreams."

"They are his dreams too. Have hope, strengthen your heart."

"Don't patronize me. You are all fools, including Rashid and Faraj. But no, I must be a good wife, loyal and unquestioning, support my man regardless. I'll support nothing that puts my son in danger. Faraj can fly after his dreams all he wants, but not me, I won't follow. I will get my son out of this place if it takes the last of me."

Mama seemed to have boundless anger; all it needed was a word, a gesture, to come lashing out. Moosa seemed to know this; he kept his eyes on the table. She paced the room.

"Inflating his chest," she said under her breath, then louder, "Inflating his chest," as if the first time was a thought, a rehearsal of what was to come. "Yes, that's what you do when you sit at his feet, reading and rereading to him the newspaper articles that you know kindle the fire in his heart, urging him on, pushing—always pushing—and if the printed words weren't hot enough you would add in your own bits, because you need a hero, you need someone to pluck you out of your own failures, a pair of strong hands always there to rescue you and send you to places you don't belong, to be something, to prove to your good father that in the end you were right to go against his will, that unlike everyone else you don't need a university degree because you were destined for greatness, riding the wave, clutching the coattails of history, while all along you knew that the man you chose to lead you was no hero, but an ordinary man, a family man, inflating his chest, making him think he had powers he didn't have, that he could face the volcano, and you—what did you do?—beating the drum that urged him on, nudging him forward, forward."

She sat opposite Moosa. I was sitting between them. The kitchen table was still covered with breakfast. And suddenly she laughed. It was astonishing to hear her laugh at this moment.

"Even the location of the flat," she said, "your *headquarters* on Martyrs' Square, was your idea. How indiscreet! It's hardly out of the way, hardly *underground*, now, is it? Wasn't it you who told him that one day it'll be a museum?" Moosa stared wide-eyed at her. "I remember now how you put it: 'Like Sigmund Freud's home in London,' you had told him, 'like Constantine Cavafy's flat in Alexandria, where people have to pay to enter,' stoking the fire. 'Had to be conveniently located,' you had argued. How considerate of you. That's what I call forward planning!" she said and laughed alone. We waited for her to stop.

I held my stomach, doubled over and began rocking.

"What's the matter?" Moosa asked.

"This is a new habit. Whenever he's upset he does this," Mama told him, her voice distant, banished by anger or grief.

But it wasn't a new habit. I had done this for a long time, she knew I had, to stop myself from talking, from repeating the things she had told me when she was ill, the things that upset her to hear, the things she made me promise not to tell a living soul.

"What's the matter, Slooma?"

"Leave him," Mama told him. "He'll stop when he gets tired."

My mind escaped to a memory: Baba was sitting reading a book by the light, I beside him. I had tried to snuggle into his side, but his body didn't give, didn't arch over me the way Ustath Rashid did over Kareem on the bus back from Lepcis. His jallabia was unbuttoned, and through it the hairs on his chest sprouted like little curled wires. I said something, but he didn't react. I rubbed his earlobe. His breath was steady and rhythmic. I pulled one of the hairs. He still didn't react. I took hold of a few and pulled them as hard as I could. The skin around them stretched out and slowly pulled them back from my grip. He held his breath for a second but that was all.

Later I asked him, "How come you didn't feel any pain when I pulled your hair?"

"When did you ever do that?" he asked.

"Earlier today, when you were reading."

"Your father feels nothing when he's reading," Mama said, then after a cold silence added, "He loves his books more than anything else. One day they'll come to burn them and us with them."

Baba left the room. I looked at Mama for an explanation. Then we both heard him slam the door to his study shut.

I began to rock faster. I couldn't stop my lips quivering, I had to suck in air.

"He's crying," Moosa told her.

"Why did you burn Baba's books?" I yelled. "Baba loves his books."

For a moment neither of them spoke. I sensed guilt in their silence. Then Mama said, "It's not like you didn't participate." I must have looked at her in horror because she said, "I saw you standing there, watching Moosa working the fire," then turned to Moosa for confirmation.

Something boiled in my throat, and like an explosion I

yelled, "I'll tell Baba when he comes home that you burned his books, I swear I will."

"It's for Baba's own good," Moosa said. He was beside me now, standing on his knees the way he did a few minutes before in front of my tin bucket on the roof, my favorite bucket with the picture of a Greek family waving and smiling in an olive grove, blackened now with soot and ash, ruined forever. He tried to whisper something in my ear. I pushed him.

"You are crazy. Crazy!"

"Be quiet," Mama said. "Behave. This isn't how I taught you to speak to your elders."

I covered my face. Moosa carried me to the bathroom. "Calm down, Champ," he said and began washing my face with cold water. I sighed deeply. He held his handkerchief to my nose and said, "Blow." He combed my hair with his fingers, kissed my hand and shook it, as if to say, "Firm up, Champ." Then, looking into my eyes, he said, "We mustn't tell the men coming here about Baba's books. You must promise."

I inhaled deeply and said, "I promise."

Then the doorbell rang, over and over, in Baba's special ring.

9

"Baba!" I said and shot past Moosa. I was first at the front door.

"Hello, Slooma," he said, walking right past me. "Where is your mother?"

There was so much I wanted to tell him, I didn't know where to start.

He slapped his hand into Moosa's. Moosa asked him something, and Baba answered, "God willing, God willing. Where's Najwa?" then looking at me, "Where's your mother?" It had been a long time since I had heard him call her Najwa. Mama walked through the hallway swing doors. Something was different about her. He kissed her on the cheek and I noticed then that she had combed her hair and painted her lips. She must have run to her room when she heard the doorbell.

"I have been so worried," Mama told him, following him into the kitchen.

"Baba," I said, "Moosa and Mama burned your books."

Baba looked at Moosa. "Did you burn everything?"

"Yes, Baba, even your papers."

"What did you do with the ashes?"

"We buried them."

"Well done," Baba said and patted Moosa on the shoulder. I was confused. Why wasn't he furious?

"You shouldn't be here," Moosa said. "We think they are on their way."

"I am leaving now," Baba said confidently and walked to his bedroom. Mama and I followed him.

"I saved your dream notebook," I said, pulling it from beneath his pillow. "I didn't let them burn it. See?" I handed it to him, but he wasn't interested.

"Can you pack me some clothes?"

"Where are you going?"

"Don't make a fuss, please, I don't have time. All of this will pass and you will see how right I was."

"They'll destroy you . . ."

"Najwa."

". . . us, everything."

"Najwa, please."

"Baba?"

"Yes, Slooma," he said, happy for the distraction.

"You need a new one. See, there's only one page left, barely enough for one dream."

"Oh yes," he said with exaggerated interest. He took the book from me and began to flick through the pages. "You know what, you are right. I must remember to buy a new one."

"I didn't read it," I said, but he was talking to Mama now.

"Underwear, socks. I mustn't forget my wash bag. Put it all in a plastic bag. I am famished."

"There's food on the table, or shall I make you something?" she said, her eyes anxious.

"No. I am in a hurry." He walked out, adding as if to himself but knowing she could hear him, "Haven't you made lunch yet?"

This froze her in the middle of the room. Then she began collecting his clothes, mumbling, "I haven't had time, and it's too early anyway, we haven't even finished breakfast," knowing he couldn't hear her. She opened his underwear drawer, her hands trembling. I stood by the door watching her, then I left for the kitchen.

I found Moosa and Baba not sitting at the table, but standing, leaning against the counter. Baba seemed excited. His cheeks were rosy and he was busy telling Moosa something. Every so often Baba would lean over the breakfast table and pick a piece of cheese or a slice of the apple Moosa had carved. There was plenty of food on the table.

Mama walked in, carrying a small suitcase, and caught him picking at the food.

"I'll make you something to take with you," she said.

"No, I must go." He slapped Moosa's hand again, and the two men looked into each other's eyes for a couple of seconds. Then he took the small suitcase from Mama, lifted it to his waist. "It weighs a ton," he said and Moosa laughed. "Do you not want me to come back, Um Suleiman?"

"No . . ."

"You want to get rid of me, I get it."

"Of course not, I just wasn't sure . . . I wanted to . . ."

Baba was already walking out, smiling broadly at Moosa.

Outside, there was a car waiting for him. Someone was sitting behind the wheel. I ran after him to the car, but stopped when I saw the driver's face and realized I didn't

know him. When Baba got into the car with the stranger he
reached above his head and pulled down the big sunglasses
that I saw him wear on Martyrs' Square. They had been
perched on top of his head all along.

★

"What did he tell you?" Mama asked, clearing the dishes
noisily.

"Nothing," Moosa said calmly, sitting at the breakfast
table smoking a cigarette.

"What do you mean, nothing?" Mama shouted at him.
"He spoke to you, didn't he? What did he tell you?"

Moosa left the kitchen.

"Where are you going?" she called after him, then in a
lowered tone told me, "Go. Make sure he doesn't leave."

I went looking for him and found him sitting in the reception room, opposite the huge photograph of the Guide.
He pulled an ashtray close to him, tapped his cigarette twice
on its rim, exhaled and said, "How are you, Champ?"

Then Mama walked in with a tea tray.

Any minute now, I thought, our house will be filled with
men from the Revolutionary Committee, turning everything
upside down, and I am not to tell of the papers and books
we burned. I remembered the book, *Democracy Now,* that I
had hidden beneath my pillow, and my skin itched with
panic.

We sipped our tea in silence. I wondered how long we
would have to wait. What if the person who had called had
got the wrong number and so hung up before speaking?
After all, that's what I would do, hang up without saying a
word. Then Moosa looked at his watch and said, "I must
go." Mama sighed and nodded in the way people do to say,

"Of course you must." Her hands were still trembling slightly.

"Do you need anything?"

"Why do you ask," she said harshly. "Didn't you just say you have to go? Well, if you truly must go, then go," she said and left the room.

Moosa sighed and went after her.

I sat for a while looking up at the huge picture of the Guide. It was impossible to ignore, so big it took over the room. The piano looked small in comparison. How long will we have to keep it there, I wondered. Then the urgent thought returned that I must find a better hiding place for Baba's book than beneath my pillow.

I went to my room, closed the door behind me, took the book out and lay with it beneath the bed. There were no photographs or drawings in it, just stacks and stacks of word lines. When I flipped through the pages all I could see were blocks of black print, separated by the occasional white space. I remembered Nasser, how once he tried to teach me to type on his typewriter. I was slow, and he was impatient. On the first page someone had written something, a dedication: "To my eternal friend and comrade, Faraj Bu Suleiman el-Dewani. With my undying loyalty, Rashid." It was a gift from Ustath Rashid to Baba. I didn't like seeing my name there. Why wasn't he content with just Faraj el-Dewani? Above my head the mattress bulged through the gaps between the wood beams of the bed. I got out, lifted the mattress and hid the book beneath it. This way, I thought, even if Mama came to change the sheets she wouldn't find it.

★

I climbed up to the roof and looked down on Ustath Rashid, Auntie Salma and Kareem's house, their curtains drawn and still, the garden silent and empty. There were days when the two houses seemed as one. Ustath Rashid would be with Baba in his study, Mama with Auntie Salma in her kitchen, and Kareem and I in the street, silently calmed by the knowledge that our fathers were brothers, our mothers sisters.

I went out to the street and found Kareem standing alone, throwing a blade into the dirt.

"Where have you been?" he said, and I immediately felt guilty. I had withdrawn from him ever since his father had been arrested, I was sure he had noticed.

The sun was shining brightly above us, but my teeth were chattering.

"Are you all right?" he asked.

I nodded and suddenly felt myself close to tears. A place in my chest ached as if something sharp was pressing into it. I felt an infinite longing for nothing specific, as if a void in my soul was announcing itself. My throat tightened and I thought if Kareem put a hand on my shoulder I would explode. He might then think I was a crybaby, a girl, so I bit on my teeth and nodded again.

"Do you want to play My Land, Your Land?" he said.

This was the first time in a week, since his father had been taken, that Kareem had wanted to play. So although I wasn't in the mood I took his blade and drew as wide a circle as I could around myself. My shadow was directly beneath me, it was noon. I divided the circle into two equal halves, his land and my land, and gave him the knife handle first. He was still observing my drawing, and even though his face was serious it was approving. We stood outside the circle and began. My Land, Your Land was our favorite

game; Kareem and I played it often because all it required
was two players, a good blade and the dirt beneath us.

Kareem was good at most games and it was always easy
losing to him, not only because he was older but more because he would never show that he enjoyed his victory. In
fact, on winning, a look of regret often cast itself on his face.
Although I was much younger than Kareem, he always
treated me as an equal. Yet there was always the acknowl-
edgment on my part of the three years that separated us: I
sought his advice, and when there was a dispute between
him and any of the other boys I always took his side.

His first throw was bad, the knife fell flat on its side.
Mine was good, the blade left a clear mark on Kareem's half
of the circle that meant most of his land had become mine.
That determined the first game, and luck stayed with me for
the next two. I beat Kareem three games in a row. This had
never happened before. Never before had I been so confident in my throws; before the knife left my hand I was certain of success. The tightness in my throat had eased and
tears were the furthest thing from my mind.

Osama, Masoud and Ali joined us.

"You let a boy beat you?" Masoud said. This was made
worse because Ali usually repeated what his brother said.
"You let a boy beat you," he echoed.

Then Osama too teased him, saying, "Serves you right
for befriending a child."

"I am not a child."

"Of course you are," Kareem said, with an irritation that
made the betrayal harsher. "He seemed grumpy, so I let him
win," he told them.

"You're a liar," I heard myself say.

"Who are you calling a liar?"

"Losing three games in a row is shameful, but to lie about it and say you let me win, well, that's just not right. No surprise there, I suppose," I said, feeling a dark, unstoppable force gain momentum.

"What's that supposed to mean?"

"Come on, Kareem," I said, looking at the boys and letting a smile escape me. "Everybody knows about your father."

"What about my father?" he demanded, taking a step toward me.

I studied my fingers. "People are talking." If I could have pulled those words back I would have, but they were out and I had committed myself.

"And what are they saying?" he said through gritted teeth. His narrowed eyes fixed on me, they were impossible to ignore.

"Everybody knows your father is a tr—"

Kareem leaped on me. His weight threw me to the ground. He didn't punch, we didn't roll on the ground, he just kept squeezing his arms around me. I remember thinking: what if I wasn't going to say "traitor," Kareem; what if I was going to say another word that started with the same two letters? You would have leaped on your friend for nothing then. Osama pulled him off me. Kareem's face was so red he might have been crying. Only a few minutes before it was I who had feared crying in front of him. Masoud pulled me up and dusted my back, slapping it a little too hard. I thought, perhaps in his house, with his fat and certain mother, his powerful and well-connected father, such firmness was always necessary. I noticed then that in one hand Kareem was clutching the knife. He could have stabbed me. He still loves me, I thought. We are still friends.

"He's younger than you," Osama said. "You can't fight him." It was the only time I was thankful for Osama's strength. "If you want to beat him, beat him in My Land, Your Land." Then matter-of-factly he added, "It's the only way."

Sensing Kareem's hesitation, I said, "I dare you."

"Go on," Masoud and Ali urged him.

"I don't feel like it," he said, his voice low and trembling now.

"Coward," I said.

He tried to charge at me again, but the mighty Osama held him in his place.

"If you are a real man," I said, "you should prove it by playing My Land, Your Land."

"Yes," Masoud said. "There's no other way."

Ali repeated his brother's words with an earnestness that made him look ridiculous.

Kareem stared at the two brothers scornfully. I remembered then what he had once told me about Masoud and Ali: "two baboons that mirror their gossiping mother in every way, even in the way they wiggle their fat bums when they walk." I recalled how much we had laughed then, and how out of character it was for Kareem, who rarely mocked anyone, and how that made me feel privileged somehow. And when I relayed his words to Mama she laughed and repeated them to Baba, who smiled broadly, his eyes gleaming with pleasure, causing me to feel proud of my friend's wit and accuracy.

He stepped out of the circle drawn in the ground and aimed the knife.

"How's the beloved?" I heard myself say.

"What beloved?" the boys asked.

"Shut up, you little swine."

"Tell us, tell us, who is she?"

"Her name is Leila."

"Not the one in his class?"

"Not the smart one who always sits in the front row?"

"Yes, that one," I said. "He can't stop dreaming about her."

They laughed. Kareem stared at me.

"Every time he heard a love song he would go all soft in the stomach for her. He told me!" I said, pointing at him.

Osama and Masoud slapped their thighs and each other on the back. Ali tried to imitate them. Kareem hurled the knife so hard its blade was entirely buried in the dirt. It was a good, clean throw.

"Listen, you, you have no word, you are not a man because you have no word." His words left his pursed lips like small explosions. I thought I saw tears in his eyes. He turned and walked away. I remembered him walking like this toward his house to comfort or shout at his mother after his father was taken. Like then, we all watched him in silence.

Then I heard myself call after him: "Crybaby!" But not even that made him turn around. "Girl!"

After he had vanished inside his house, the boys looked at me. I pulled Kareem's knife out of the earth, erased the circle with my foot and said, "I don't know why he's so upset. It's only a game."

Osama, Masoud and Ali said nothing. It was lunchtime anyway. We all went to our houses.

10

The Revolutionary Committee Mama and Moosa were expecting, those for whose sake Baba's books were burned,
never did come that day. We ate lunch expecting them,
cleared the table expecting them and went to have tea in the
sitting room expecting them. Moosa was still there. He
didn't leave to do the things he said he needed to do. I went
to my room, closing the door behind me. I sat on the foot of
the bed and thought about what had happened with
Kareem. Voices in my head started telling me off:
  "You know what you've done, don't you?"
  "You know it or do you need us to tell you?"
  "You betrayed him."
  "That's what it was: betrayal."
  "There's no other word for it."
  "Why, Suleiman? Why did you do it?"
  "You are wrong about yourself."

"You are a terrible person. You thought you were good, always believed it, but the truth is that you are a traitor."

"Traitor! Traitor!"

"Remember what you wanted to be, dreamed you would be, were certain you would be, for Mama, for Baba, for Moosa?"

"An airplane pilot. An art historian like Ustath Rashid. A great pianist, although you hated the piano, with a black tailcoat that you would flick behind you before taking your place to play in one of the great halls of the world, just so that you could see their smiling faces in the front row, looking up at you."

"Like kissing Baba's hand in front of his friends, you imagined these things too would make your chest glow with happiness and pride."

"How many times you imagined their eyes gleaming with pride!"

"But you were wrong about yourself."

"You have always been bad. Just waiting for your true nature to rise."

"You see how bad you are now? This is only the beginning."

"Things only grow in this world."

"What you are now is what you'll forever be."

"One's nature is like a mountain, you can't change it."

"The only difference is, unlike a mountain, one's nature grows."

"The devil has found a home in you."

"And when the devil finds a home it likes, it never leaves."

"Warm, comfortable, he sleeps in your belly."

"When the Day of Judgment comes, when all that is

unseen will become visible, your heart will be seen for what it is: empty and cruel."

"As empty as a rotten chestnut."

"Your deeds will be visible then in Eternity."

"You'll never feel the pleasure of that secret warm glow smoldering in your heart, that warm glow that is goodness."

"Do you remember it tickling your chest every time you kissed Baba's hand?"

"Or when Kareem entrusted you with his secret love for Leila?"

"You loved that, didn't you?"

"Yes. 'He's twelve,' you said to yourself, 'and I am nine, but he has entrusted *me* with his secret.'"

"And you betrayed him."

I felt the first sting of tears in my eyes. I hoped they would come.

"And why did you betray him? Could you say why?"

I shook my head to say no.

"You can't tell him you didn't mean it."

I shook my head again.

"You can't say it was an accident."

"A slip of the tongue."

"No," I heard myself say, and heard the tremor in my voice.

"You meant to hurt him."

"No," I said again.

"You did."

"You even enjoyed it; admit it."

I nodded.

"But Kareem is your best friend."

"Yes," I whispered, and the tears fell.

"Oh, Kareem is certainly kindhearted. 'You can see it in

his face how white his heart is.' These were your words. Traitor!"

"Traitor!"

I buried my face in my hands.

★

After a while I came out and washed my face. Moosa had left. I saw Mama getting ready to take a nap, pulling the curtains shut, turning on her bedside lamp. She didn't notice me. When she was about to turn around I moved out of view. An excitement rushed through me. I thought this must be how it feels to be a police officer or a thief in one of those American films.

I went to watch television in the sitting room. I sat on the floor, cross-legged, only centimeters away from the screen. A man was sitting in a chair in a room. I turned the volume up slightly. The upper half of the wall behind him was the color of sand, the lower green. It was chipped in several places, showing white beneath the paint. The man looked thin. He faced slightly to one side. His knees were touching, he looked like a schoolboy in detention. He wore a white shirt under a gray jacket. His clothes seemed too big, his shirt collar almost touched his ears. His cheeks were gray with stubble. Suddenly, and with such speed it was dizzying, the camera zoomed in on his face, moved left, right, until he was in the center of the picture, then focused. A light was shone on him. His eyes squinted against it. It was Ustath Rashid. I waited for him to speak. Another voice mumbled something. I turned the volume up a little. It seemed that Ustath Rashid, too, didn't hear what the voice had said, he tilted his head slightly to one side. A shadow of a big hairless head fell on the wall behind him. The voice repeated the question:

"Were you present at the meeting?" Ustath Rashid nodded, then said, "Yes, I was present." But the word "present" was barely audible. He was asked to repeat. "Present, present," he said. "Who else was there?" Ustath Rashid looked again at the man with the hairless head. "We will read a list," the voice said calmly, "and you will answer yes or no." I heard the sound of shuffling paper before the voice spoke a name. Ustath Rashid hesitated, looked at the shadow, the shadow came closer, his head becoming bigger on the wall. Tears gathered in Ustath Rashid's eyes, he looked thirsty, his Adam's apple rose and fell, then he nodded. More names were read out, and Ustath Rashid continued nodding, sometimes before a name was even fully read. Then I heard Baba's name: "Faraj el-Dewani?" It was strange to hear Baba's name on television. Ustath Rashid hesitated a little. He looked to one side, his stubble made a strange noise against his shirt collar. The voice reread the name, this time inserting "Bu Suleiman" into Baba's name, which again, like when I had read it in the book Ustath Rashid had gifted Baba with his "undying loyalty," made me feel implicated, dragged by my name into something I knew nothing about. Then Ustath Rashid spoke. He said, "No."

I ran to Mama, but found her asleep. I knelt beside her bed. "Wake up, Baba's name is on television," I whispered. Her cheek was resting on her hand, her lips distorted, her breath came and went in deep swings. She was overperfumed. I felt the urge to slap the air beside her.

I returned to the television. The screen was covered now in a still photograph of pink flowers. This was the picture that meant the broadcast was temporarily interrupted. I heard it said that the Guide had a switch in his sitting room, beside his television set, so that whenever he saw something he didn't like he flicked the flowers on. I sat and watched the flowers, hoping Ustath Rashid would come back on. I wondered if Kareem was watching. I had seen such interrogations before broadcast on television. They are meant to show the nation the "faces of the traitors." Ustath Rashid said, "No," when Baba's name was mentioned. I knew that this was the opposite of betrayal.

I ran back to Mama. I put my nose beside her distorted lips and was certain that she had had some medicine before sleeping, maybe after I saw her draw the curtains and turn on the bedside lamp, maybe before, maybe while Moosa was still here. Maybe he, too, was made to swear on her life not to tell a living soul? I felt anger blister my cheeks. Her medicine bottle was beside her. It was as big as a water bottle and had nothing written on it, the liquid inside it the color of water. She had left it standing open on her bedside table. Without thinking I took it to the kitchen and began pouring it down the sink. I stopped to imagine what she would do when she found out. She could always go to Majdi the baker and buy another, I thought. I emptied it all.

At this point the doorbell rang. Whoever it was kept their finger on the bell. The continuous ringing didn't wake Mama; she didn't come running toward the door, anxious, saying, "Coming, coming." By the time I was halfway down the hallway I heard myself shout, "Take your finger off the bell." I was surprised by how quickly my order was obeyed. I looked through the peephole. It was Bahloul the beggar. His head, his long and knotted hair and beard, straining to hear. When I opened the door he hesitated, looked like he was almost going to leave.

"You haven't given me any money lately," he said.

"Not now, Bahloul. Mama's asleep and Baba's on a business trip. Go away."

"You are rude. You plant nothing for the hereafter. A kind word is a seed you'll find as a tree in the hereafter."

I couldn't think of anything to say. A strange exhaustion came over me.

"Feed me," he said.

I let him in. Bahloul had never been in our house before. When he was out of the sun, in our hallway, I smelled him and saw how dirty his jallabia was and how black his bare feet looked against the carpet. His toenails were like bird beaks or things made of wood. "No," I said and pushed him out. I was surprised by how easy it was to get rid of him, how willing he was to obey me. It made me feel guilty. So I said, pretending that it was my plan all along, "Go around the house. I'll let you in through the kitchen." When he didn't react, I added, "It's better this way," and closed the door in his face.

If one family refused to give Bahloul money, he talked about them, said they were "mean, greedy, shortsighted; they think Heaven is near" and things like that. He told everyone that he was saving to buy a small fishing boat, but after he got the boat he continued to beg. Um Masoud said, "Of course, it's easier to beg than work. The boat was an excuse, now he's got it—paid for out of our money—he'll find another reason to beg, the lazy cockroach."

By the time I had reached the kitchen he was already standing at the door, his nose touching the glass, steam gathering below it. He must have run, happy for my kindness. I suddenly felt affection toward him. I let him in. I took out some bread, cheese, honey, and poured him a glass of milk. He ate slowly.

"There's a strange smell in here," he said.

My skin itched. I remembered I had promised Mama not to let anyone in the house when she was ill. I silently mouthed the same prayer over and over, one I had heard Moosa say before: "Concealer, conceal our faults."

Bahloul saw my lips move. He screwed up one eye, pointed his finger at me and said, "I see you, I see you." He peered around the room suspiciously. "You haven't let the devil in, have you? When the devil enters, he clings to everything."

"Come on, Bahloul," I said. "Hurry up."

"Give me some money."

"I haven't got any money."

"I get no help from you. How am I ever going to become a fisherman?"

"You have already got your boat."

"You are shortsighted. You must do for the hereafter as you do for today. Fishing boats are expensive. Or don't tell me you've believed Um Masoud's rumors? They are lies, partly true of course. All lies have the truth in them somewhere, but still, thanks be to God, no lie is ever completely true, not really. I've got the boat, that's true. But I swear on the Prophet's grave that it hasn't touched water yet. It's swimming on sand. I sleep in it. I have no money to buy nets. I need nets to trap the sea." He took a sip of milk, the edge of his mustache turned white. "Serious business, fishing." Then his eyes fell on the medicine bottle I had just emptied. He slowly floated toward it, sniffed it, then stared at me. I grabbed his hand and begged him: "Don't tell, please, please. Promise on your life that you'll never tell a living soul, ever." He looked at me as if I was going to bite him. His hand, dark and flaked with dirt, as coarse as bark, began to tremble. I squeezed it and said, "Promise."

"Protect me from the devil," he suddenly yelled toward the ceiling. I fell back. "God!" He screamed like a horse and shot out to the garden. "Protect me from the devil, keep him at bay."

I ran after him. He ran around the house several times, like a trapped animal. I chased him. On one of his laps he noticed the garden gate as if for the first time, he thought of returning to it, but when he saw how close behind I was, he yelped and bypassed it. His jallabia filled like a balloon against his back. I dropped to the ground, breathless. When he appeared again and saw that I was now sitting in front of him, he yelped again, turned and shot in the opposite direction. I grabbed a handful of stones and hurled them at him. One pierced the balloon of his jallabia and made a deep satisfying thump on his back. He screamed like a horse or a monkey in the jungle. He wrapped his hands around his head, hunched over and hopped a few times. I found more stones and threw them at him. Every time I missed my anger hardened. Bahloul found the gate and escaped, screaming and running down Mulberry Street.

I had never frightened anyone so much before. I watched him run, reach the end of the street then turn right toward the sea, toward his home, his fishing boat in the sand. I was suddenly frightened by what he might do the next time we met. Perhaps then he will understand that there was nothing to fear, that I am the boy and he the man, I thought.

I sat on the pavement for a while, drawing lines in the sand with my finger. I am sure Bahloul won't tell, he'll be too frightened to speak, I thought. When I realized how hot my head had become, I went back indoors.

11

Something in me was ashamed of what I had done to Bahloul. It was the first time I had heard a grown man scream like that. I was glad no one had witnessed it.

I went to see Mama. Her room was dark and smelled of sleep, but she wasn't in bed.

"I am here," I heard her say from the sitting room. "Where have you been?" she said, facing the television even though it was still showing the photograph of the pink flowers. Her tone, the way she sat stiff and unmoving, immediately unsettled me. This was a mood that overtook her at times, one I was familiar with, and which turned her in search of conflict. "Why did you pour the bottle down the sink?"

"I didn't know what it was," I lied. "I thought you wanted me to clean the bottle."

She sighed and lit a cigarette, throwing the lighter on the coffee table. "I see you don't need me. You are quite capable of feeding yourself on your own."

She had mistaken Bahloul's food, still on the kitchen table, for mine. What a relief, I thought. I stood there for a few seconds, watching her back stiff in the air, her knees touching, her cigarette burning in one hand in front of her face, wondering what I could do to untangle her. Her eyes remained on the pink flowers. I wondered when the Guide would switch the broadcast back on. I imagined him in his pajamas, drinking tea, going to fetch something, or deciding to go for a pee and on his way flicking on the switch that controlled the broadcast. How will we find Ustath Rashid now, I wondered. Will he be sitting on the chair, or hand-cuffed on the floor, his cheeks crimson, a heroic drip of blood from one corner of his mouth? I thought of telling her about him, how he was sitting, as still as she was now, fac-ing the camera, squinting against the light. And how when it came to Baba's name he didn't give in to the big man with the hairless head but said, "No." What heroic chords that word caused to resonate in my ears! It reminded me of a film that told the life of a group of African slaves in America. At one point the slaves threw down their tools, stood in silence and slowly, like a drum beaten to announce something dreadful, clapped their hands together in unison. Slaves clapping to their white masters, I thought, makes no sense. But when I looked behind me I saw Baba poised in admira-tion. Something in Ustath Rashid's "No" reminded me of that solemn standing ovation the slaves had given to their masters. As soon as the flowers came on Ustath Rashid was probably beaten, I was certain he was "taught a good les-son," "his face spared," as Moosa had said about those in-terrogated on television, but his body a "patchwork of bruises." I was surprised the telephone hadn't rung. At other times when we saw someone we knew interrogated several people would call to say: "Did you see? So-and-so was on television." I was certain that because it was aired during naptime, when under the full glare of the sun the whole world went to sleep, no one had seen it. Even Kareem and his mother probably missed it. I was probably the only one in the world who had seen it, I thought. I was suddenly thankful for the pink flowers and wished for them to stay until Ustath Rashid's interrogation was over.

"Call the bakery," she ordered. "When you get Majdi, give him to me."

Sometimes when Mama was unwell or busy she got Majdi to deliver bread and, if we were alone, her medicine too. She called out his number and I dialed it. When Majdi answered, I said, "Just one moment, Mama wants to talk to you." He didn't say a word. His silence seemed to know, as if he was expecting the call. I imagined his earnest face, his hand poking beneath the wide flour-sprinkled counter, looking about him before bringing out a bottle wrapped in black plastic.

"Good evening," Mama said. "I need two loaves." There was plenty of bread in the kitchen, I knew this when I served Bahloul the food. "And, yes, one bottle." Her cheeks blushed. "No, no. One will be enough," she said in an artificially formal tone.

When Majdi arrived she sat him in the reception room because it's impolite to just take what he had delivered from the door and leave it at that. He looked uncomfortable to be there. His blue jeans were dusted with flour, his hair made gray by it too. I remember thinking I couldn't wait until I had gray hair, although I knew his wasn't really gray, that when he showered all the flour would wash out to leave his hair black and ordinary. His hands clutched the armrests in a way that made me think of what Bahloul had said: "When the devil enters he clings to everything."

Barely a minute had passed when he stood up and said he had to go. Mama paid him and walked him to the door. She then went to the kitchen, the black form of her medicine bottle stood on the kitchen table. She threw an impatient glance at me. We sat in an uncomfortable silence. I began to tap my foot against the leg of the table. "Stop," she said. I felt as awkward with her now as I did when I had to keep a guest company in the reception room while she made tea. She lit a cigarette, and I went to my room.

I lay in bed, curling myself beneath the sheet. Going to bed in the middle of the afternoon had always felt strange, but now it seemed right somehow. Outside, I heard her walk to her room, a liquid being poured into a glass, the familiar chinks of ice. I remembered the cigarette that was burning in her hand. Mama only smoked when she was ill and then she didn't allow one cigarette to die before lighting the next. Sometimes she would forget and have two going at the same time, one in the ashtray, the other between her fingers. I was nervous she would fall asleep while smoking. Several times I had woken up in the night to make sure all the cigarette butts in the ashtray beside her were out, looking under the bed in case one had fallen there. That was one of the reasons why I couldn't leave her side when she was ill. I heard her move around the house. I could tell she was bored. She often, during those empty days when Baba was away, walked aimlessly around the house. And she never sang to herself in that soft, absentminded way she often did when taking a bath or painting her eyes in front of the mirror or drawing in the garden. That singing that had always evoked a girl unaware of herself, walking home from school, brushing her fingers against the wall: a moment before the Italian Coffee House, a moment sheltered in the clarity of innocence, before the quick force that, without argument, without even the chance to say, "No," thrust her over the border and into womanhood, then irrevocably into motherhood. I wanted so much to make her happy, as happy as she seemed when Baba was home. Except it wasn't happiness that came over her then but something like confidence: she moved faster and sounded more self-assured. Could I ever come to inspire that in her, I wondered from beneath the bed sheet.

★

I had faded into sleep and woke up disoriented, not knowing what time it was. The sky was dark, the world was silent. But still I felt a warm comfort at having napped for the first time. I must be becoming a man, I thought. I noticed an odd smell in the house, but the tide of sleep was strong, it pulled me and I drifted back into the warmth and magic of its certainty.

A few hours later I woke up dying, horses galloping up my nostrils, down my throat. I jumped out of bed and opened the window. I did this in every room of the house, opening windows and doors without knowing why. She had left the gas on in the kitchen.

When she woke up the following morning she couldn't understand why I was so upset and kept repeating, "What's this smell, did you leave the gas on in the kitchen, Slooma?"

I slammed the door shut and locked myself in my room. From the way she spoke through the door it felt as if it really was another woman who had left the gas on to kill us.

"Why are you upset at me? How do I know you are all right if you don't speak?"

My mouth was about to utter something, but I held it shut with my hand.

"How do I know that you are not dead?"

I covered my ears and shut my eyes.

"OK," she came to say in the late morning. "At least come out for some food. It's almost lunchtime and you haven't even had breakfast." When she walked away, I heard her say to herself, "What a strange boy." After a while she returned to ask, "What if your father comes home now, what will he say about us?"

By noon she slipped a note beneath my door. It read:

> I, therefore, hope that my beloved son will honor me with his visit, and I am sending my vizier to make arrangements for the journey. My one and only desire is to see you before I die. If you refuse my request, I shall not survive the blow. May peace be with you!

It wasn't funny. I recognized the words. They weren't hers, they were from a letter King Shahryar had sent, when his heart was ill with sadness and he believed he was going to die, to his brother King Shah Zaman. She just replaced the word "brother" with "son." I folded it twice and pushed it back beneath the door. After a few seconds I heard her pick it up.

By the afternoon knives were stabbing at my stomach, and I was dying for a pee. I walked out and went straight into the bathroom, locking the door behind me. I couldn't hear her outside. I went to the kitchen, poured myself a huge glass of milk, grabbed a loaf of bread and went straight back to my room, leaving my door ajar. It was past four, naptime was over. Where was she?

I went out onto the street to see if any of the boys were

there. I found them all gathered around Adnan. Adnan was the only one who had been absent when Kareem and I had fought. If he had been there, I might have behaved differently. I was certain that Osama, Masoud and Ali were now telling him their version of the story. Kareem was leaning on a car. When they saw me they stopped talking. Ali said hello and Masoud stared at him. They had all agreed, I thought, to ignore me. "Let's go and see the school," Masoud told them. But it wasn't a school day, it was summer. To my surprise they all followed him. I watched them walk away. Osama put his arm around Kareem, talking to him as they walked. Adnan walked beside them, listening to Osama. When they reached the end of the street and turned out of sight, I began to follow, walking slowly, kicking a pebble, digging my fists into the pockets of my shorts. I turned after them and they were in view again. In the distance their figures looked closer together.

When they reached the school gates they stopped. Just before I caught up with them Kareem shouted, "Last to Mulberry is a girl," and like a herd they came running toward me. When they were close I thought of getting out of the way, but I suspected they were trying to frighten me so I didn't move. I closed my eyes and stood still, making myself as thin as possible, listening to their panting, feeling the wind from their speed brush past me. And I heard Kareem shout again, "Last to Mulberry is a girl," and I knew he meant me.

Adnan had remained by the school gates, weak with illness. He was as old as Kareem but couldn't run very far. He wasn't allowed to eat any sweets, and if his skin was punctured he was in danger of losing all of his blood. He had to take two injections a day, and he gave them to himself. Once we convinced him to show us. "If you laugh, I'll slap each one of you," he warned before taking us into his bedroom. None of us had ever been inside his house before. He had books on his disease that occupied a whole shelf. He had a huge dictionary open on his desk with a perfectly sharpened yellow pencil in its fold. Without a doubt it was the biggest book I had ever seen. Small brown medicine bottles clustered together on his bedside table. Each bottle had his full name, Adnan el-Melhi, handwritten on its label. His room was spotless, and his bed was made so tightly I wondered if it was comfortable. He had an entire box of syringes in his desk drawer, and another with miniature yellow sponges in plastic envelopes. "These disinfect the skin," he explained.

"Why?" Ali asked.

"What do you mean, why?" Adnan snapped at him. "So that no germs enter me, of course."

We all crowded around him. He pulled down his trousers, rubbed his skin with the sponge, then without introduction drove the long needle deep into his buttock. None of us said a word. He pulled it out and pressed the small yellow sponge in its place. His buttock was dotted with brown bruises. We never wanted to see him do that again.

I envied Adnan. His illness had earned him a peculiar sort of strength and gained him something none of us had: a private world that involved books and syringes. His room was like a little house, with things that belonged only to him. And although the bruises on his buttock made me thank the Healer for my well-being, I also prayed for a disease that would give me what Adnan had, that thing that made him seem older and more independent than any of us and led us all to silently seek his approval, the approval of the only one among us who, with his own life and literature of illness, seemed to need no one. This is why, if he had been present the day before, I probably wouldn't have betrayed Kareem. Adnan had that sort of effect. The fact that he was closer to death aged him and gained him a higher moral authority. Like my heroine, Scheherazade, he, too, was living under the sword. And so the challenge—"Last to Mulberry is a girl"—didn't apply to him.

Adnan placed his arm on my shoulder. I continued to stare at the empty schoolyard, our dark green flag draped under its own weight on the high pole. I remembered how we used to stand every morning in parallel lines under the weak winter sun, our schoolbags dense on our backs, screaming the national anthem to the lazy flag, competing with the scratchy music that blared out of the gray, cone-shaped speakers fixed to each corner of the yard, high enough so none of us, even if piled on another's shoulders, could reach them. Some mornings I stood so erect, tightening my fists and flexing my back, feeling tears sting my eyes as I sang our national anthem so loudly I had to spend the rest of the day trying to swallow the sore left in my throat. Other mornings I stood half asleep, miming the words, trying to hide my yawns under the cacophony.

Adnan pulled at my sleeve and together we walked back to our street. He didn't say anything, but I knew he was trying to comfort me. We could see the boys gathered by the entrance of our street, panting. Osama, who always won these races, leaned against the lump of stone that had the name "Mulberry" written on it. Ali was standing beside his brother, looking unhappy. He always came last, he must have been whacked on the head by everyone and called a girl. They were all looking down our street at something

Adnan and I couldn't see. When we reached them I whacked
Ali on the head and called him a girl. I had no right, I hadn't
taken part in the race. Still, I wasn't satisfied so I whacked
him again and called him a girl three times. He tried to hit
me, but it was easy to hold him off with one arm. Adnan
pulled me to one side and with his shoulder nudged me
away. When we were out of earshot he said, "Is your father
home?" Adnan rarely asked me a question, I couldn't help
but feel flattered.

"He's on a business trip," I said.

He looked ahead and said, almost to himself, "That's
lucky," and walked on, his step much livelier than usual.

Beyond him I saw the same white car that had taken
Ustath Rashid. This time it was parked in front of our house.
"That's the same car . . ." I heard one of the boys say from
behind. I wondered what Kareem was thinking. I expected
him to rush beside me, take hold of my arm and say, "Now
we are one, brother." Adnan walked past the white car, looking only at the ground, pushed the garden gate to his house
open and let it swing shut behind him. I could see only one
head in the car. I looked back. All the boys were gone except
for Kareem. He stood still, looking at me. I wanted to run to
him, but turned instead toward the car and began walking
forward. I tried to think of Scheherazade, her bravery, but no
matter how hard I tried I kept hearing Mama's words: "You
should find yourself another model. Scheherazade accepted
slavery over death." I thought of Sinbad, but I never liked
him because he was a thief. I thought of the slaves clapping
in unison, but they had one another, one person clapping
wouldn't do; besides, hadn't they also accepted slavery over
death? I was close now to the car. The man spotted me in his
side mirror. When I reached his window and saw his face,

I froze. I remembered him. He was the one with the old woman's voice who had stood in the doorway of the sitting room, blocking the way, looking down at me sitting on the floor beside the tray of food, shaking my head and waving my hand close to my chest as if to say, "It's not me, I swear, it's not me," the one who had slapped Ustath Rashid, the one who had followed Mama and me from Martyrs' Square. His skin was etched with small holes, like tiny chisel marks. His eyes were narrow and the white in them dull. His lips were dark, as if they were painted with blue dye. He could have been eating mulberries or drinking blood. Tight curls formed a helmet on his head. He smiled at me.

"Suleiman," he said lazily, as if my name was chewing gum in his mouth. "We meet at last."

I couldn't stop looking into his eyes, a strange force within them seemed to be pulling me. I thought of the flames of Hell Eternal licking the sides of the Bridge to Paradise, how they will seem like a familiar voice to the unfaithful who will turn toward them the way you can't help but turn when you hear your name called, because, as Sheikh Mustafa said, "Fear enters the hearts of only those who have a cause to fear."

"Who are you?" I asked.

He placed his palm against his chest and said, "My name is Sharief. I am a friend of your father." I knew he was lying. "You don't remember me?"

"You searched our house."

"Yes. I needed to ask him an important question." He faced forward and smiled to himself. He almost looked embarrassed. "I suppose I was in a bit of a hurry."

"So you weren't going to take him away like you did Ustath Rashid?"

"Ustath who?"

I pointed at Kareem's house. "I saw you."

"Oh," he said as if it was something he had just remembered, then laughed. "No, no, no. Your father is not like that. He's a good friend of mine. We have known each other for years, like brothers really. In fact, it was he who sent me to see you. I had heard so much about you, Slooma."

I knew he was lying, but how did he know my nickname? I remembered the way he had pushed Mama's medicine bottle against her stomach. He knew our secret, I thought, knew it and chose to keep quiet. "Is Ustath Rashid a traitor?" I asked.

"Yes," he said without hesitation.

"And Baba, is he . . ."

"That's why I am here. I am trying to defend him, but I need evidence." The word "evidence," so full of needles.

"Is that what you wanted to search for?"

"Exactly."

Unlike Mama and Moosa, he answered my questions. He didn't treat me like a child.

"Where's Baba?"

"I can't tell you," he said, digging in his pocket. "He asked me to give you this." He handed me one of Baba's English fiery mints. I took a step toward him. Then, on the seat beside him, black and fat, I saw a gun. I stepped back.

"Come, come," Sharief said calmly in his thin, coarse voice. And I did. I walked to him. He handed me the gun, handle first, and said, "Here, touch it." As I extended my hand, he said, "Men are never afraid. And you are a man, aren't you?" The gun metal felt as cold as a dead fish. He placed it on the seat beside him and said, "Here, take the candy, it's from Baba." My head was practically inside the car now, and the smell of old socks and cigarettes made me dizzy. The weight of the stench struck me as a sign of man-hood, and so there was some excitement in being so close to it. Perhaps to be a man was to be heavy, I thought. The V of his safari jacket revealed the beginning of his chest. His skin was brown-red from the sun, glazed in sweat. Anyone seeing us like this would have thought us friends. I took the mint. Kareem was gone. Did he leave in disgust when he saw how close I and the man who had taken his father were becoming, I wondered.

"You know, it is very bad what your mother is drinking," Sharief said, looking at me with half a smile, his eyes almost regretful. "She could go to jail."

He could see from my expression that I understood. I wanted to beg him not to tell.

"Her secret is safe with me."

I was so grateful I could have kissed his hand.

"But you, Suleiman, will have to help me."

"Anything, anything."

He looked ahead, smiling. "I require a list of Baba's friends, as many names as possible, to vouch for him."

My mind raced to remember. "Can't I vouch for him?"

He laughed. "No."

"Why?"

For a moment I thought he was annoyed, then he smiled again. "We need men, adults," he said and the smile vanished. "Come on, Slooma, you must know at least one name."

I nodded in the way people do when they are busy searching their memory but wish to offer you a silent assurance that they are close to arresting whatever it is that was now clinging to the tip of their tongue. At that moment if a name was unlucky enough to be remembered it would have been spoken, given up. I thought of the book below my mattress. "I can't remember any names," I said.

"What do you mean, you can't remember? Try." He was irritated. His breath was hot and smelled of rust.

My body trembled. I was surprised at how close to tears I was. "I have a book," I heard myself say. "I saved it from the fire."

Then I heard my name being yelled. It was Mama. I saw her pale face inside the shade of our house, standing in the hallway. I ran to her. As soon as I was inside she slammed the door shut. She went down on her knees and gripped my arms hard. "What were you doing with that man? I saw you, don't lie." She tightened her grip. I never saw her so frightened. "What has he been telling you? Is this the first time?" I pushed her and ran. The moment I pushed her I heard her give a gasp, the sound of it made me see a small red balloon ebb in the sea's deep blue. When I entered my room I recalled it several times, and every time it made my heart ache. I wished she would come after me. I wanted to apologize. I wanted to show her what the man had given me, the English fiery mints that Baba bought on his travels; it had to be his because it couldn't be found in our country.

12

I found her sitting at the table, smoking. I sat opposite her. I
wanted her to say something, to even repeat, "I saw you,
don't lie," but she ignored me. I watched the garden through
the glass door, its floor brushed long with shadows. We can
go up to the roof and see how the sea changed today, I
thought. Or I could set up her drawing table in the garden
where she liked to draw an orange, a plum, a twisted leaf. I
never had the patience to sit for her, but now I was willing
to try.

"He had a gun, you know. He let me touch it." Her eyes
looked up at me. "I wonder what Ustath Rashid did? Do
you think he's a traitor, do you think Um Masoud is right? I
know she gossips a lot, but I've been thinking about it and I
think it's true: there *is* no smoke without fire. Well, it's true,
isn't it? Can you have smoke without there being a fire? You
can have steam, but that's different, isn't it?" She didn't say
anything. She looked at me, then took a quick, nervous drag

from her cigarette. Her fingers trembled slightly. Smoke spilled from her nostrils. "He said he was a friend of Baba. He even called me Slooma and gave me this." I put Baba's English fiery mints on the table. Mama's face began to change. The moments before we cry the face tries to fold away, hide itself from the world. "He said Baba will be home soon. Please don't be sad."

Sharief didn't say that Baba would be home soon, nor did he say, "Don't be sad." Those were my own words that I put in his mouth, like Moosa adding in his own bits to the articles he read aloud.

She mumbled something. It wasn't until she cried again that she repeated it: "Stupid Faraj."

I thought of saying, "Baba isn't stupid" or "Don't call Baba stupid," but she left the kitchen. I heard her bedroom door slam shut and the key in it turn. Then the telephone rang in the sitting room. She unlocked her door and ran to answer it.

"Hello? Hello? Who is it?" she said rapidly, then her eyes fixed on a spot on the wall and I guessed someone was talking at the other end. "Yes, Bu Nasser, I am Um Suleiman." She turned around herself. "Bu Suleiman isn't here." She looked at me, pursing her lips and shaking her head slowly. "With all due respect . . ." she said and was interrupted. "With all . . . With all due respect, Bu Nasser, this has nothing to do with me." Then after a moment she added, "Nasser is old enough to make up his own mind. You ought to take this up with him." She looked at me again, raising her eyebrows, shaking her head. "But I have just told you, Bu Suleiman isn't here. I have no idea where he is. Listen, I am sure Nasser will be fine," she said and quoted from the Koran: "'Say: Naught befalleth us save that which Allah hath decreed for us.'" Then she listened to Nasser's father. "Well, Bu Nasser, if you feel this way, you should tell your son. No one is forcing him to work for my husband." When she put the receiver down she kept her hand on it, then telephoned Moosa. "Can you hear an echo? Good, neither can I. Listen, Nasser's father has just called. He's worried. He wants to know how involved his son has become. Says if anything happens to him he will hold Bu Suleiman personally responsible." She looked in my direction, turned around and began secretly whispering. "And there was an echo in the line. Yes, of course I know what that means. Call Nasser and tell him what his father said and tell him that I am upset: his father threatening us, holding us responsible for his son's fate . . ."

I suddenly remembered what Judge Yaseen had said to Baba after Moosa quit university: "You have ruined my son."

"OK, good-bye," Mama said and hung up. She went to her room.

A little while later the telephone rang again and she came out, not running this time but walking with confidence and the air of authority possessed by those who believe they are innocent and right. She almost answered it, but something stopped her. She snapped her fingers and, as if the person calling could hear us, whispered, "You answer."

I picked up the receiver and looked up at her. "Hello," I said.

"Slooma." It was Nasser. There was an echo; it was a bad line. "It's Nasser here."

"I know," I said.

"How are you, young man? How's your mother? Can I speak to her?"

I handed the receiver to Mama. She pressed her hand against the speaker, curled her eyebrows and whispered, "Who is it?"

"It's Nasser," I said and began walking away.

"Listen," she whispered. "Was there an echo in the line?"

"Yes."

Biting her lower lip she gently placed the receiver down. I didn't ask why she did that, or why she was still standing beside the telephone. After a few seconds it rang again.

She snapped her fingers again and said, "Tell him I am not here, then hang up, don't chat." She walked back to her bedroom.

I picked up the receiver and said, "She's not here."

"Why did you hang up on me?" Nasser said. He sounded hurt; his voice, trembling slightly, was made strange by the echo in the line. After what seemed an endless pause he said, "When she returns tell her I called, OK? And . . . And tell her also that I am sorry about my father, about what he said."

I never understood why I had taken a dislike to Nasser from the moment I had met him. Why was I always short when he was always nice? When he called on Eid to wish us good health and happiness he always insisted on talking to each one of us. Baba would hand Mama the receiver, smiling as if he was embarrassed or proud, as if this Nasser was his creation, as if he was responsible for everything Nasser said. When it was my turn I always tried to get out of it, but Baba wouldn't agree to tell him I was in the bathroom or out playing in the street. He would tense his eyebrows and motion for me to take the receiver from Mama. Nasser always spoke in the same way, calling out,

"Slooma!" as if I was on the opposite side of the road, then, "How are you, young man?" I answered all of his questions as briefly as I could, and when he wished me good health and happiness I wished him the same, and when he said, "I am your friend, Slooma" or "If you need anything, think of me as your older brother," I didn't know what to say and so said nothing but, handing the receiver back to Baba, I always felt a strange rush of anger burn my cheeks. And hadn't I many times wished for an older brother, an older brother like Kareem or even like Nasser?

I suddenly felt a warm glow of affection for the first time toward Nasser. I felt bad that I had lied to him, so I said, "It was Mama who told me to tell you she isn't here."

I thought I heard him chuckle, try to restrain a laugh. But then he shouted, "Who's laughing? Are you laughing at me?"

"I am not laughing at you," I said, but whoever was laughing was now laughing even louder so Nasser couldn't hear me.

Through the laughter I heard him shout again, "Who's laughing, I said?"

"What's your family name, boy?"

"Suleiman Faraj el-Dewani."

"Not you," the voice interrupted. "You, the one called Nasser. What's your family name? Speak?"

This was not unusual. Many times it happened that I was speaking to someone on the telephone and a third person would come in. And sometimes I was that third person, hearing two people having a conversation, one voice always farther away than the other, and sometimes I couldn't resist listening in, and once or twice I made background noises of stormy winds and explosions, and once I played them songs by Boney M. What was unusual about this was how, even though everything said was succeeded by an echo, both Nasser's and the stranger's voices were equal in volume. And because in life—as Baba had told me—you can't listen and speak at the same time, the echo of my voice returned strange and new, and I realized that I had never heard myself before.

"Don't speak to him, Suleiman," Nasser ordered. "Hang up, hang up now." He sounded desperate.

"This Nasser character isn't very friendly, is he, Suleiman," the voice said calmly. I laughed because what he said sounded funny in contrast to Nasser's desperation. The returning echo of my laughter sounded sinister.

"Don't listen to what he tells you. Hang up, I said," Nasser shouted.

I heard the other voice say to himself or to someone else beside him or maybe to me, "This Nasser character likes to play games."

"Hang up!"

"No, I am not hanging up, you hang up if you want." My words traveled between them like an arrow, uninterrupted.

The voice exploded in laughter again. Nasser's line went dead. The voice stopped laughing and listened with me to the unending dial tone. After a couple of seconds, just when I was about to hang up, he said, "You are wonderful, boy." I didn't know how to respond. "Tell me," he said in a way as if we were old friends. "How's your mother? You have such a beautiful mother, you know." I felt my neck stiffen. Then he laughed and repeated what I had said to Nasser, *It was Mama who told me to tell you she isn't* . . . , and laughed again. My heart quickened and time seemed to slow down. "Ah yes," he said, catching his breath, "what a beautiful mother you have. Great tea she makes, wonderful harissa. There's nothing like homemade harissa." I suddenly recalled how on the day she minced the red chili peppers Mama would bar me from entering the kitchen because of how the heat, she said, could burn my eyes. She wore gloves and wrapped a scarf around her mouth and nose like a robber. "You should be thankful for a mother like that. Are you thankful, Suleiman?" I nodded twice. "Tell her that if she ever needs drinking company, to call on me. Tell her I too get my medicine from that scoundrel, Majdi. Thank God for Majdi."

I threw the receiver down. My heart raced like a mouse trapped in a wheel. I stood stiff by the telephone, unable to move. It rang again.

"Hello," I said, hearing the tremor in my voice repeated by the echo.

"Slooma?" It was Nasser. He was whispering.

"Nasser. Thank God it's you. Who was that man? How come he knew us? He knew things nobody knows. Who is he?" We were brothers now.

"Did you hang up on him like I told you to?"

"Yes."

"Good boy. Now listen, there isn't much time, I need you to give a message to your mother." He was still whispering. I didn't like him calling me "Good boy" but I had never felt such affection for Nasser as I did now. "Tell her that we are doing all we can to find Ustath Faraj, we don't know where he is, he hasn't turned up here." I imagined him speaking from the flat on Martyrs' Square. "We have been expecting him . . . Do you know where he is?"

"Why don't you stuff this telephone up your arse, fucker," the voice returned again.

"Hang up, Suleiman," Nasser shouted, and this time I hung up immediately. But as soon as I did, the telephone rang in an odd continuous ring. Fearing it would disturb Mama, I picked it up. It was the same man. His voice was clear, the echo now gone. "Listen, boy. Do you know Nasser's family name?" I said nothing, but then he shouted, "Speak up."

"No," I said, remembering Ustath Rashid's interrogation on television.

"Do you know where he lives?"

"No." Then, fearing what he might say next, I said, "Yes."

"Good," the man said and I thought it was over, but then he said, "Look, Suleiman, this is how this works. You will tell me where Nasser lives, and I will write it down. OK?" I felt my head nod, then, as if he could see me, he said, "OK."

After a short silence he shouted, "Speak, boy."

"You know where Martyrs' Square is?"

"Yes," he said so softly it astonished me.

"He lives in one of the buildings there." Then in a lame attempt at retreating I said, "I think. I am not sure."

"But of course you are . . . sure," he said with confidence. I was confused. The pause before the word "sure" seemed so deliberate I wondered whether he meant of course I was *not* sure, or of course I *was* sure. "And which building on Martyrs' Square are you not sure he lives in?" he said.

"The one right on the square." His silence was heavy, so empty I felt I had to say more. "It has green shutters. His is on the top floor, with a red towel on the clothesline in front of the window."

"Good," the man said. Then he added, and again I didn't know whether he was speaking to me or to someone else beside him or even to himself, "The red towel, that's the code, the bastards."

"Nasser is a very nice person," I added. But he had hung up.

13

The afternoon was lending itself to evening. Mama lay in her room dozing. I lay in my bed and, although I couldn't see him, I knew that Sharief was still there, loyal, waiting in his white car, the sun dimming around him, hoping I would remember names or bring the book I had mentioned and place it in his hands, the book that was still beneath my mattress, beneath the place where I slept and dreamed. The book had begun to annoy me like a stone in my shoe, and I felt I couldn't rest until I gave it to him or got rid of it somehow.

The window in my room was open. From where I lay I could see the sky blue and solid above the white garden wall made golden by the sun, the line where they met red and black, a trick of the light. Staring into the sky often made me thirsty; now it was causing a place in my chest to tickle. I wondered how it would be to fly, to be inside the solid blue.

One day Baba will take me with him on a business trip, I was certain. I will dress in a suit and tie and walk beside him like a shadow, his "right hand." When we board the plane I won't be impressed because flying will be normal to me by then. We will sit and not even look out of the window, busy with more important matters written in long slim columns in newspapers. I will then be a man, heavy with the world. I imagined my life without Baba, I imagined doing all of these things alone, and the tickling in my chest stopped. I hardly ever did something alone with Baba, and to give up this one fantasy saddened me. He was away so often, and when home he was usually distracted by a book or a newspaper. I was perplexed whenever I caught him looking at me with longing.

The only activity Baba and I did alone was the walk together to the mosque on Fridays. Although Mama never herself prayed or insisted that I did, she was still proud to see me dressed in my white jallabia and cap, holding Baba's hand, musked and ready for prayer: a miniature replica of Baba. I didn't look forward to Friday prayer and was always happy when it was over, but I did like the walk with him. I remember holding his hand and squinting against the bright noon sun, our white jallabias glowing in the heat. He was always silent during these walks, no doubt refraining from speech in order to listen to the Koran as it blared off the minaret speaker, recited by Sheikh Mustafa, too loud to be understood. Many times during the prayer I remained standing while all the worshippers bowed. Watching the entire place change color, I felt frightened to be the only one in the world seeing them like this: a carpet of hunched white backs like seagulls grooming their chests. After the prayer

Baba enjoyed introducing me to his friends. They thought it sweet that I was dressed like him. I never went to prayer when Baba was away.

When he was home, Baba seemed distant. Away he seemed closer somehow, more alive in my thoughts. For this reason it was strange when Mama merged us together. She did this by using the plural form of "you." "You always leave me alone," she would say, after I'd come in from playing in the street, meaning both of us, using the you that made Baba and me inseparable. It obliged me to defend him, to say, "But Baba is working hard for us," when I had no idea whether he was working hard for us or not. I defended him because I was defending myself. But I know now that that, of course, made us indistinguishable, the man who was her punishment and the boy who sealed her fate.

Sometimes she would say, "All you men," "All you men are the same," combining me not only with Baba but with many other men. I never knew what to say to that. I couldn't possibly defend all of them: all her brothers and her father—the men she called the "High Council"—the men who met to decide her fate when she was only fourteen, after she was seen sitting across from a boy in the Italian Coffee House. And all the other men who met at the Italian Coffee House, where talk started and things were decided. These were the men who were bound to talk if she wasn't married at once. The men whose threat of talking made my grandmother say, "If a slave came to propose, a slave as black as this night, I would give you to him." Those were the men the High Council imagined gossiping in low voices, saying, "Look, look who's over there, sitting with a boy, and touching hands under the table, now above the table, daughter of a good family, the shameless creature, the boy is blushing like a pig, has more shame than her," in the Coffee House, the Coffee House from where shame was going to fall on everyone in the good family if they didn't act quickly, if they didn't marry her at once, even to a slave. She had told me the story so many times of how she and Baba came to be married, of that "black day." Every time she would leave something out or remember something new. "It was because I was so beautiful," she sometimes began, or, "It was all because of Khaled, that stupid uncle of yours. He was the one who gave me up, betrayed me; the dagger was his."

Khaled was Mama's brother. He had left for America to attend university, and everyone missed him. When I was born they asked him to choose a name. "Suleiman," he had told them, "after Suleiman the Magnificent." Later he returned with an American wife who didn't like the taste of our water. Her name was Cathy, she smelled like no one else in our country, a mix of eucalyptus and grass. She was the reason why I had for a long time imagined America as a forest. She used to bring a book with her when the family gathered. She didn't join the women in the kitchen, but sat alone and read. I once heard Auntie Nora, Mama's only sister, whisper that what Cathy was reading was her Holy Book. But I didn't think she was because the book had a picture of a woman in a sleeveless dress running from a man in a dark suit and hat holding a gun.

I once saw them, Uncle Khaled and Cathy, argue under the glue tree in our garden. He slapped the tree, and she covered her eyes with one hand. Soon after that they returned to America. I missed Cathy. I liked having someone with yellow hair in my family. The boys used to elbow me and giggle whenever she visited us.

Before America and Cathy, Uncle Khaled lived in Tripoli and wrote poems that half of the family was ashamed of and the other half loved. When I asked Baba what he thought, he said, "A great poet, your uncle. Very important." And the only time I heard Baba shout at my grandmother, the one who had swallowed the entire book of *A Thousand and One Nights*, was when she had neglected Uncle Khaled's wooden trunk of papers. She put it in the chicken shed, where the clever chickens picked at the lock and ate all the poems.

"Ignorance!" Baba shouted. Then, "Ignorance! Ignorance! Ignorance!" he repeated like a bell.

My grandmother seemed perplexed, perplexed and slightly embarrassed, as if someone had farted loudly in the room.

"Don't raise your voice at her," Mama told him.

"Are you happy now?" Baba said. "The only copy of *The Feast of Ants* is inside the chickens."

The Feast of Ants was a play Uncle Khaled had completed before he went off to America. It took him seven years to write and it read like a long poem, telling the history of our country.

Mama said, "Feast or no feast. Don't raise your voice at my mother again."

Baba looked at Mama, then at my grandmother, then at Mama again before he left the room.

When Uncle Khaled returned from America and found out that his poems and *The Feast of Ants* had been devoured by the family's chickens, he laughed, then laughed some more and laughed again until his laughing took him out of the house and to the end of the garden, where he sat for a long time alone not laughing. He refused to eat an egg laid by those chickens the whole summer. "They are full of poetry," my grandmother teased. He smiled but didn't eat.

Mama blamed Uncle Khaled for that black day she was

forced to marry Baba because of what he had done when, on one of his visits from America, he saw her and her friend Jihan in the Italian Coffee House drinking cappuccino with two boys. Mama and Jihan were fourteen years old, so were the two boys.

"The coward. Thinking himself the enlightened American. He was nice. Cordial. Said hello as if he admired his little sister and her friend. The foolish girl I was; I even thought, with his liberal ideas, he was proud of my little rebellion. He paid for our cappuccinos, said hello to my friends. When he left I cried with happiness and told Jihan how much I loved my brother. Having a brother like him was the only thing in my life that in any way resembled Jihan's life." Jihan was Mama's childhood friend, a Christian from Palestine. Her parents treated her the same as they did her brothers. "Talk about a rude awakening. When I got home every light in my life was put out. The High Council was already adjourned. Oh yes, when it comes to a woman's virtue, we are fierce. Fierce and deadly. And when it comes to a daughter's virtue we are fierce, deadly and efficient. In such matters our efficiency rivals that of a German factory." A smile crossed her face and was gone. "Your grandmother grabbed me by the hair and threw me in my room. 'You have shamed me, you little slut. Now your father will think I haven't brought you up right.' I didn't know what she was talking about. It was like a nightmare, no sense in it at all. But soon I learned that the poet-prince had run straight home after seeing me at the café and told his father, 'Your daughter is fourteen and is already spending her days in cafés with strange men. I tremble to imagine what next. Marry her now, or she'll shame us all.' 'Strange men'? They were boys, just boys. 'Tremble to imagine'? Only a poet would have the cruelty for such a phrase."

When she identified me with them, saying, "All you men are the same"—saying it and looking away from me as if at that moment the mere sight of me repelled her—I didn't defend Uncle Khaled and all of those other men, but felt a hot anger burn in my belly. And at night, after she had stopped talking and shouting and smoking and had fallen asleep somewhere on the floor or in a chair where I couldn't lift her, couldn't carry her, because I was only nine, and instead took myself to bed, not caring whether I had brushed my teeth or washed my face, I lay there in my clothes and shoes like a traveling cowboy picturing how I could have saved her then, when she was fourteen, before what happened happened, falling asleep fighting and shouting and running away somewhere beautiful and green and cold like Scotland, where no one could ever find us, surrounded by silent cows with big, beautiful, glassy eyes.

At such times I hated our house.

And some nights what I imagined wasn't good. I fantasized revenge, enacting it over and over until the black sky broke gray with dawn. It filled me with urgency. I couldn't wait to be a man. And not to do all the things normally associated with manhood and its license, but to change the past, to rescue that girl from her black day.

★

The sun was on its way down, burning warmly now on the white wall of the garden. The solid, cloudless blue seemed eternal. Lying on my side, I shielded my eyes, placing one hand against my forehead, the other between my knees. This is how the Bedouins sleep. Baba's family were Bedouin. He, too, slept like this: one hand over the eyes, the other between the knees. It must have become a habit to him in the days before he left for university, before he left the place of great expanses and scarce shade, before becoming a suited *afandi*. And me, I wondered, what reason is there for me to sleep like this? How much of him is there in me? Can you become a man without becoming your father?

14

The following morning Bu Nasser arrived and wouldn't let his finger off the doorbell. I opened the door and he walked in.

"They took my boy. Where's your mother?" When he saw Mama he said, "The catastrophe has fallen. I called you yesterday to prevent it. Now it's too late." He spoke the way some women do when they arrive at a funeral, swaying from side to side.

"Calm down and tell me what happened," Mama told him.

"I looked everywhere, Nasser has vanished."

Bu Nasser was much older than I expected, perhaps as old as my grandfather. Instead of opening the curtains in the reception room and letting in the heat, Mama put on the light. "Suleiman," she said, "fetch your uncle a glass of water." I waited for him to do what all guests do when offered something, to refuse, but the old man didn't say a word, he must have been very thirsty. I stood outside of the entrance, listening.

"He was there, beside me, when I telephoned. He got upset at what I had told you. He always gets upset at what I say, said exactly what you told me, that he was old enough to make up his own mind. But," whispering now, he added, "Um Suleiman, this is a dangerous path. These people have no mercy." He sighed, then said, "I was only blessed with two, a boy and a girl. Nasser is from the Precious One, may God have mercy on her soul. The girl is from the second marriage, she's only nine, young enough to be Nasser's daughter. He's our only shelter in the world."

Throughout all of this Mama put in a few good wishes: "May God reward you. May He bless them."

Then a girl walked timidly into our house. The main door must have been left ajar after the old man walked in. She had long chestnut hair, her skin was cinnamon from the sun, and her lips slightly open and purple-pink. She must be Nasser's sister, the one who is nine years old, I thought, exactly my age and therefore too old for me to marry. The acceptable age difference had to be at least three years. Baba had been my age when Mama was born, old enough to walk into her family home bearing flowers for the new arrival. He was twenty-three when he married her, she fourteen. With such a gap no one could object or say she would grow barren and old before he did. Because you had to think ahead. A woman had to be young and strong enough to bear children and serve the man well into his old age, so that her locks would remain black as coal when his head was bald as the moon. She looked at me and saw exactly what I was doing. She shut the door behind her, louder than was necessary.

"Who's there?" Mama said.

"Come. We are here," the old man said. Then softly to Mama he added, "It must be Siham, my daughter."

Siham walked into the reception room.

"Didn't I tell you to wait in the car?" the old man said.

"But why?" Mama asked him, in a way to welcome the girl. "Why sit out in the sun when she can be here with us. Come here, sit beside me. Mashaa Allah, Mashaa Allah. You are so pretty. What school . . ."

I ran to the kitchen. I giggled to myself for some reason.

"Slooma," Mama called.

I ran there but just before I had reached the reception room I stopped and walked in slowly. "Yes," I said calmly, hearing my heart thump.

"Come say hello to Siham, she's Nasser's sister. Slooma is so very fond of Nasser," she told them. "Aren't you, dear?" I felt my cheeks blush at her calling me "Slooma" then "dear" in front of them, in front of her, Siham, the one with the chestnut hair.

"What would our young bride like to drink?" Mama asked. Siham said nothing. She didn't seem embarrassed, more withdrawn. "How about some Coca-Cola?"

"Speak up," her father said, irritated.

"Yes, please," Siham said. Her voice had a bodily pleasure, like the sun warming your skin after a swim in the cool and calm early-morning sea.

I left to bring her the Coca-Cola—I had completely forgotten about the old man's glass of water—but then her father ordered Siham to go with me. And so there I was, walking side by side with Siham along our hallway, feeling my chest glow with the excitement that moments ago had caused me to jump around the kitchen. I held the hallway swing doors open for her, then followed her through.

"You were eavesdropping," she said. These were the first words Siham had spoken to me. I made myself busy with the Coca-Cola. But then she rescued me. "I too like to eavesdrop."

"Would you like to see my workshop?"

She shrugged her shoulders. "Is it far?" Her eyebrows rose slightly.

"No," I said. "It's on the roof. And it has shade too." I handed her the glass of Coca-Cola, filled to the brim.

She brought her mouth to it and slurped. "Aren't you going to pour one for Baba?"

I remembered that the old man wanted a glass of water, but I was too embarrassed to admit to her that I had forgotten, so I poured him Coca-Cola instead and walked quickly to the reception room.

I had often dreamed of this, but up until this point the girl in my dreams had only been the girl Mama once was, before what happened happened, before she was forced into marrying the man who was to become my father. It was an infinite longing, hideous and unbidden, beyond reason or fulfillment, like a sick dog gnawing at its own limbs. But this was sweet.

I handed the old man the glass. I had spilled some on the way, making my fingers and the glass sticky. "Put it there," Mama said, pointing at the coffee table. "The line was tapped, so I didn't take his call. I thought it better this way. Better for him, I mean," Mama said.

"He left in a hurry, annoyed at me, didn't even say good-bye. I am sure he went to that wretched flat on Martyrs' Square."

The words caught my ear. I stopped outside the entrance.

"I went looking for him there. My heart shuddered when people told me they had seen a young man run across the square with a typewriter under his arm, chased by a group of Revolutionary Committee men."

I felt dizzy, sick.

Once I had skipped school with this other boy. I don't even remember his name, we weren't friends, the only thing that had united us was the desire to skip school. When I was caught and flogged with a bamboo stick on the front and back of my hands, I lied and told them it was his idea. It didn't feel wrong at the time, but when he eventually was brought into the room and saw me I felt terrible. I had betrayed him. This felt the same. How could I ever marry her now when I had betrayed her brother, the man who was to be an uncle to my children?

I walked back to the kitchen, dragging my feet. She wasn't there. Her glass stood empty on the breakfast table. The door to the garden was open. I walked out and found her there. She looked irritated. "Where have you been?" she said. "It's this way," I said, leading the way up the staircase to the roof, my head lowered. I hadn't imagined it to be like this. "This is my workshop," I said. The roof was ablaze with morning sunlight, my tools strewn beside the water tank now that my bucket was ruined.

"Baba says your father has brought ruin on my brother's head. I love my brother. Your father must not be a very nice person."

"Nasser is like an older brother to me," I lied. Her eyes kept squinting at the roof. "I, too, love your brother." The air was still. I put my arm around her shoulders and caught the smell of oranges. She turned away and ran down the steps.

When I reached the reception room I found her standing between her father's knees.

"What's the matter, darling?" Mama asked her. "Who upset you?"

I stood at the mouth of the room, frozen, my skin itching with shame.

"Slooma, what did you do to Siham? Did you upset her?"

Siham said, "I know who that is," pointing at the huge picture of the Colonel. The shoulders of his military suit glittered with golden decorations. The sky behind him cloudless, the blue luminous and sweet like candy.

Mama suddenly excused herself. I didn't want to be left alone with them. When Bu Nasser wasn't looking at me, I watched him and his young daughter staring up at the photograph. He was too old. He will probably never see her marry; her children will probably never see their grandfather. I ran after Mama.

She was kneeling before the safe, dialing the code, mumbling the words Bu Nasser had told her: "'The catastrophe has fallen. I called you yesterday to prevent it.' Why come, then? What do you expect me to do?" The safe didn't open. She was dialing it too fast. There is no margin for error: any slight variation on the secret code and the safe wouldn't open. She tried again, repeating what she had said before in front of me and Moosa, "Children playing with fire." The heavy steel door swung open, indifferent, mighty. She took out a stack of ten-dinar banknotes and rolled them up tightly into her fist.

They were still staring up into the photograph of the

Colonel. But when we walked in the old man stood up and said, "We must leave now."

"Stay for lunch," Mama said with such insincerity the man didn't even feel the need to reply. "Honestly," she said. "Stay." But the old man, holding Siham's hand, was already walking toward the door. "Honestly," Mama repeated, following them out. The old man shook his head and patted his chest. Siham mimicked him. Seeing her imitate such an old person's gesture saddened me. Then Mama quickly reached for the man's chest pocket. With amazing speed the old man clinched her wrist. His quick reflex was surprising, as if he had lived his whole life ready for attack. Then the usual argument ensued:

"I swear you must."

"No."

"But for my sake."

"There is no need."

"OK, then, if not for my sake, for Siham's."

Siham looked up at the two adults and, closing one eye against the sun, she patted her chest again. The gesture inappropriate now.

The man hesitated. Mama saw the opening and stabbed the money into his pocket. "I swear by what you hold dearest . . ."

The old man froze for a moment, then, like a man defeated, he shook his head dejectedly.

"You have no idea how dear you all are to Bu Suleiman," Mama told him.

He walked beside his daughter to their old black car. As they drove off they revealed the Revolutionary Committee man, Sharief, sitting in his white car, not minding the heat, loyal to his cause, his gun probably still occupying the passenger seat beside him. His confidence and youth were in stark contrast to the sad old man. Sharief seemed beyond age and need, a man calling for the world to keep up with him.

Mama pulled me back into the house. Every time I turned around she said, "Come on, come on." Before she closed the door, I caught Sharief waving at me. Mama turned the bolt twice.

15

The following day Mama woke up not so much happy as certain. She began to make a cake. She was silent the whole time, moving quickly and precisely. I thought, At last she and Auntie Salma are going to make up. But after she decorated the cake with strawberries she took it across the street to Ustath Jafer and Um Masoud's house. I stood in the doorway, watching her. Sharief, too, watched her from inside his car. He had become a fixture, it no longer surprised me to find him there. She pressed the doorbell, quickly glancing at Sharief, and with her fingers outstretched rubbed a flexed palm against her dress. As if she was at a loss what to do, she waved to me to come. Just before I took hold of her cool and moist hand Um Masoud opened the door.

"Hello," Mama said, a soft quiver in her voice. "Is Ustath Jafer in? Please, I need to talk to him. About a very important matter." Then, handing Um Masoud the cake, Mama said, "I made you this."

★

That visit has remained with me ever since. Whenever I am faced with someone who holds the strings of my fate—an immigration officer, a professor—I can feel the distant reverberations from that day, my inauguration into the dark art of submission. Perhaps this is why I often find a shameful pleasure in submitting to authority. Even in prayer—bowing down, my forehead pressed against the ground, my back arching beneath its own weight, my chest falling between my shoulders, my hands flat against the ground, fingers pressed tightly together, hearing my own whispered prayers—I am often overcome with regret and, yes, shame that I am gloating in it, enjoying my own deprecation. And this is also why, when I finally think I have gained the pleasure of authority, a sense of self-loathing rises to clasp me by the throat. I have always been able to imagine being unjustifiably hated.

★

Ustath Jafer, like most government officials, kept us waiting. We sat in the reception room, where the face of the Guide stared down at us from a photograph that was much smaller than the one Moosa hung in our house. The room was done up in the color of the revolution: the walls pale green, the furniture upholstered in darker green fabric, still covered in plastic, so that when you squirmed it made the sound of a fart and you had to squirm again to prove that you hadn't farted. A small coffee table stood in the middle, where it couldn't be easily reached. On it there was an empty ashtray and a tissue box with one pink tissue shooting out of it, closely followed by a yellow one. The curtains were drawn—they were also green—and a weak light burned in a small chandelier above the coffee table. A huge television stood in one corner; it was perhaps as large as my piano. Mama sat upright, her knees touching, her hands wrestling with each other: every time the blood rushed back into one she would rub it out again. Um Masoud walked in and sat beside her.

"He's coming," she said.

Mama looked at her and nodded.

"Why trouble yourself with the cake?"

"It's nothing."

"We are neighbors . . ." Um Masoud started, but then to my astonishment Mama began to cry. Um Masoud didn't seem surprised; she must be used to this, I thought. "In fact I have been thinking, saying to Jafer," she went on, "'why doesn't she come when she knows we can help?' I know we haven't always seen eye to eye but . . ." She leaned toward the coffee table and plucked the pink tissue.

"I wanted to . . ." Mama said, taking the tissue from Um Masoud's swollen fingers.

"Never hesitate, we are sisters."

"I swear to God," Mama said, "I have always liked you." Her eyes wide open, eager to convince.

"Don't worry," Um Masoud said lazily. Her confidence was repulsive. "Men are like that. They like adventure. The Guide knows this and he is very forgiving."

"Really?"

"Yes," Um Masoud reassured her, then, lowering her voice to a whisper, added, "Let me tell you this. Once a man was fixed on killing him."

"Really?" Mama said, assuming disbelief.

"Yes. What can you say? Mad. His mind had left him. When he was caught, the Guide sat with him and asked,

'Why did you want to kill me, my son?' They say the man melted like ice in fire, weeping for forgiveness, and the Guide forgave him there and then." Mama looked astonished, hopeful, ridiculously naive. Um Masoud plucked the yellow tissue and handed it to Mama. "I don't mean to brag, but Jafer has a special place in the Guide's heart. And Jafer is, of course, heart and soul devoted to him. Yes. After all, isn't all of this good fortune we are in," she said opening her hands toward the ceiling, "because of his generosity? It wouldn't be right to bite the hand that feeds you."

"Of course," Mama said, adding in the way people do at weddings, "May God nurture the goodwill and keep the envious at bay."

"From your mouth to God's ear," Um Masoud said.

★

Ustath Jafer rarely stood chatting with any of the neighbors. He wasn't unfriendly, but kept conversations to a minimum and always assumed the air of the sort of man I would later come to recognize, one who wanted to make the burden of his monumental responsibilities clear; that he was a man who was thrust by fate's benevolent hand into the vortex of his time. He greeted people with a sort of inverted modesty that seemed designed to make them feel humble. He was always dressed in a suit and tie, his hair blow-dried and parted to carefully conceal the receding line. He wore gold-rimmed sunglasses, which he rarely took off when shaking hands with others. He didn't have to seem outwardly eager to prove his loyalty. He was a senior member of the Mokhabarat, trained in Moscow by the KGB, concerned with the larger picture, with the mechanics of security, calculating who was to remain in front of the sun and who to be fixed firmly behind it. Most of us as children were led to fear him. Most of us secretly admired his power in comparison with our parents. Not one of us didn't want to be in his shoes.

He walked into his reception room, where Mama and I sat waiting like patients at a doctor's surgery. Mama stood up, I didn't. He came straight to me, ruffled my hair and said, simply, "Suleiman."

I stood up, my eyes on Mama, hoping to deflect his gaze.

"How are you?"

"Answer your uncle," Mama said.

I faced the floor and mumbled, "I am fine, Ustath Jafer."

This made him clap his hands and laugh. He finally turned to Mama. He shook her hand without looking at her face, repeating, "Sit down, sit down."

"Najwa has come especially to talk to you, Jafer," Um Masoud said in an unnecessarily loud voice, a smile lurking on her face. "She is our dear neighbor. The Prophet taught us to love our neighbors."

"Of course, of course," Ustath Jafer said benevolently.

"Thank you," Mama said and repeated her statement: "I swear, I have always liked you," adding that, "Masoud and Ali are like my own. I swear, there is no difference between them and Suleiman." Then, to my horror, she began crying again.

Um Masoud looked at her husband and pursed her lips. She seemed to genuinely feel for Mama.

"Go and make us tea," he said quietly, and Um Masoud left the room. His tone changed when he addressed his wife, it was rough and unrestrained.

"I swear to you, Bu Masoud," Mama said, "these days are pure hell."

He didn't ask what she meant, he seemed to know, seemed to know everything.

"He's innocent. If he has done anything, it's because he was urged by others. Bu Suleiman has always been devoted, he isn't the type. It's just that other people, may God forgive them, have been whispering in his ears."

"He shouldn't have listened."

"I know, I know," she said. "But, what can you say, the devil is mischievous." Then with renewed hope Mama said, "I swear, since we found out about Rashid, we have had nothing to do with him or his family." She began to weep again. "Please, Ustath, you must believe me."

"There, there," he said so softly that I felt a strange urge to hug him. "God is great. Capable of all things."

And that was all he said, "God is great" and "Capable of all things."

The tea came, served with the cake Mama had baked. I refused to have any, but Um Masoud insisted. I held the plate in my hand and looked at it. I plucked the strawberry from the icing and put the whole of it in my mouth. "He's a sweet boy," Um Masoud said. Ustath Jafer glanced at me and shouted, "Masoud, Ali," then asked his wife, "Where are they?" They were at Osama's house, she told him, watching television. I imagined all the boys gathered there, watching one of the latest cowboy films Osama was always able to find. He had a genius for hunting down the latest videos. My heart turned with longing.

★

Um Masoud walked us out. When we were at the door she gasped. "Just a minute," she said, then returned with the piece of cake she had given me with the strawberry missing. "There, Suleiman, be a good boy and give this to the gentleman sitting there in the car." Then to Mama she added, "They work so hard, sitting in the sun all day." Mama stared blankly at Um Masoud.

Glad the cake wasn't meant for me, I took it to Sharief, who smiled past me at Um Masoud then took the plate.

The boys were coming out of Osama's house now, their eyes sleepy. They must have been watching the film in the darkened sitting room, each taking a stretch on the thick carpet, folding cushions beneath their heads, blasting the volume. When the hero had kissed the heroine they must have giggled, thrown cushions at each other.

I walked with Mama to our house, but then, when I saw the dark shade of our hallway, I decided to stay out. I walked around the garden, shook a branch of the orange tree, but no fruit fell. I went and stood on the pavement, kicking a pebble, hoping one of the boys would say something, include me in some game or conversation.

Adnan had begun to stack stones on top of one another. They were going to play Six Stones. I sat on the pavement. Sharief was devouring the cake. Just when they were ready to start playing I grabbed a pebble and threw it from that great distance to knock down the stack of stones. I wanted to impress them with my aim. But the stone hit Adnan instead. They all turned toward me. Osama, the mighty Osama, came charging at me.

"Are you mad?" he yelled. I remembered that if Adnan's skin was punctured he could bleed to death. Osama was now right in my face. "Have you lost your mind?" He thrust the heel of his palms into my chest and I fell. I heard Sharief leave his car. "Do you want to kill him?" Osama yelled, kicking me as I lay on the ground. "Enough," I heard Sharief say and I received another kick. Where was Kareem?

"I said *enough*," Sharief said and grabbed Osama by the back of the neck. "Enough means enough." Osama threw his head back to relieve the pain. Sharief pushed him toward the boys. Osama lost his balance and fell. He looked back at me with hate in his eyes. When he reached Adnan he put a hand on his shoulder, then kneeled down to inspect his ankle, the place where my stone had landed.

"You can't just hit each other over nothing," Sharief said and returned to his car, a speck of cream clinging to one corner of his lips.

I ran into the shade of our house. Mama was in her bedroom, the door shut. She must have been asleep or ill. A few minutes later I heard an ambulance come screaming into our street. I peeped out of the window of the reception room. Adnan was resting with one arm on Osama, the rest of the boys crowded around him. He limped into the white arms of a doctor, his ankle a ball of bandages. Sharief stood holding the ambulance door open. He shut it with great care.

16

The thrust of Osama's palm heels still echoed in my chest. I was sure I would bruise, that two blue shadows would reveal themselves above each nipple. I had also grazed my elbow on the hard pavement. Fear, but more self-pity, reverberated through me like an electric current as I lay on my bed. I curled into a ball on my side and recalled how the rest of the boys, clustered with concern around Adnan, had glared at me. Kareem was the only one not surprised; he had already decided, or so it seemed, on the kind of person I was. Masoud seemed shocked, but was also relishing the excitement as he fussed around Adnan's injured ankle. His young brother, Ali, did what he had always done when overwhelmed by a situation, he cried, looking repeatedly at his older brother for guidance. Adnan was solemnly attending to his wound like expected bad news that had finally arrived, neither encouraging nor objecting to Osama's attack on me. Perhaps he didn't even notice it. But Kareem, if anything, seemed relieved that day, as if something doubted had now been confirmed. Perhaps doubt is worse than grief, certainty more precious than love.

By rushing to my rescue Sharief had split the sea, created an undertow that would pull me even further away from Kareem. We drift through allegiances, those we are born into and those we are claimed by, always estranging ourselves. I recalled how, pulling me off the pavement by the hand, Sharief had sighed, "Slooma"—the sugary variation of my name used only by my family, and which I now seldom hear—whispering it almost, claiming me. And I recalled also how minutes later he had closed the ambulance door behind the horizontal figure of Adnan, his gun bulging through the split of his jacket, accepting Osama's anger, agreeing that I wasn't innocent, that Adnan was the ultimate victim and I the ruthless, or at best careless, child, puncturing the skin that can't stitch itself.

The spot on my elbow, which these days is hard and coiled like the skin around an elephant's eye, was the color of beetroot, burning but already sealed.

As I lay on my bed I tried hard to remember names. I could only think of Ustath Rashid, Nasser and Moosa. I was sure this wasn't enough; still, hope tickled my chest. I couldn't wait to run to Sharief. I lifted the mattress, took the book and ran out, silently mouthing, Rashid, Nasser, Moosa, both hands clasped tight around the book, squeezing it as if it were a fish trying to get away. But Sharief wasn't there. The boys too were gone. A circle of tire marks was drawn in the dirt. Concerned for Adnan, he must have raced after the ambulance, maybe even gave it an escort, I thought. I stood there feeling hollow. *Rashid Nasser Moosa.* The names still in my head, bubbling on my tongue, strangely unfamiliar, as if I were hearing them for the first time.

Concern. I think that was what I craved. A warm and steady and unchangeable concern. In a time of blood and tears, in a Libya full of bruise-checkered and urine-stained men, urgent with want and longing for relief, I was the ridiculous child craving concern. And although I didn't think of it then in these terms, my self-pity had soured into self-loathing.

I put the book beneath the mattress in my room and curled again on my side. I listened to the crickets that were now carving the air outside my window. The deep azure sky was weakening, gray entering it. I heard Mama walk into the room, but I pretended to be asleep. My bed was narrow, made for one person, but she found a place beside me and buried her face in my neck. She had always seemed captive, captive in her own home, continually failing to prepare herself for anything else. Her breathing became unsteady. I felt her tears on my skin, her breath smelled warm and salty, sharp with medicine.

"What am I to do?" she said. "What am I to do what am I to do what am I to do what am I . . ."

"Mama," I interrupted. Her voice was like sand rising, it scared me.

"What if they can't or won't help us?" she suddenly said.

"Who?"

"This Jafer and Um Masoud," she snapped angrily. I felt blameworthy. "I don't want to live if I must live like this."

"When I am big, I'll take you to Scotland. I promise, on my life."

Then my mind went back to the time when she was imprisoned; every fantasy about the future revived that original dream: the rescuing of the girl she once was.

"Mama, tell me what happened after Uncle Khaled saw you in the Coffee House." This was the first time I had asked Mama to talk about the past. Normally, when she was ill, I remained as silent as the wall, hypnotized and horrified.

She said nothing.

Is she thinking how to start, I wondered, or is she pretending she doesn't know what I am talking about?

She took a deep breath and began whispering into my neck. I felt a great relief wash over me. I could have listened to her forever. I wanted to turn around and hug her, but I was afraid if I moved everything would change. "Your Auntie Nora was the one who told me," she started. "She eavesdropped on the High Council's first hearing," she said and giggled that strange giggle that was somewhere between laughter and crying. I smiled, thankful to have her back on familiar ground. "It was our curse to have seven brothers. They were all gathered with your grandfather. Khaled was at the center, of course. The poet is finally listened to, finally given full attention by the 'hypocrites.' That's what he used to call them because they used to mock him, couldn't understand his sensitivity, his complex ideas, the gifted poet." She was definitely ill. But it didn't matter somehow. It was good to have her there, holding me and telling stories again. Even her medicine breath was tolerable, more than tolerable, it reminded me of the past, it was part of us now, part of the stories. Because if the past had a smell it was this, sharp, hard and piercing.

The section of the sky visible through my window was

darkening. Thin veils of cloud drifted in and were brushed orange and crimson by the setting sun taking its last deep breath before sinking into the sea. The merciful breeze that came in the early evening was gently turning around us. My limbs relaxed, and I wished, silently, deeply, that nothing would come to disturb us, that the telephone and the doorbell would remain silent. I even hoped Baba would delay his arrival. We were both captive, our house and the past our prison, but it was familiar, not full of shadowy urges and cold alienation. I remembered the boys, the ambulance, Sharief, and squeezed Mama's arm more tightly, darkly content with the world I was given, thankful to be hers, happy she was a mother because, as Sheikh Mustafa had confirmed, all mothers will enter Heaven. I was surprised how easily his words spilled out of my mouth: "'God has promised every mother Paradise because the suffering endured by women surpasses all kinds of human suffering.'"

"Once, when I was near your age," she said, "I stood talking to the next-door neighbors' boy. He had said something and I laughed. Your grandfather saw us. I still recall the lash of the hemp rope chasing me down the street, the people on the street, their eyes savagely curious, my own uncontrollable and hideous yelps, the rope making the sound of hiccups behind me, and your grandfather's mysterious silence and strained smile that he always had on his face at such times. I ran into our house screaming. When your aunt and grandmother saw him they screamed, begged him to stop. He said nothing, chased me into the courtyard. I was closed in, trapped. His hand fell with the weight of a sandbag on my cheek."

Mama's description of my grandfather's smile reminded me of Ustath Rashid's smile when he was breaking up the fight between his two students in Lepcis, and Baba's smile when Nasser called on Eid.

"Later, when Khaled told your grandfather that he had seen me in the Italian Coffee House sitting in mixed company, they locked me in my room for thirty days and rushed to find me a groom. Khaled had sentenced the flower, the young, stupid, naive fourteen-year-old girl, to life imprisonment.

"For one month I was locked in my bedroom," Mama said dreamily. "One month," her arm tightening around me. I felt such immense love for her. "When your grandmother said, 'Stay here until you have contemplated your actions a thousand times,' I thought of your Scheherazade. The word 'thousand' was what evoked the memory of that wretched woman. But, somehow, thinking of her, I didn't feel so alone. I remember promising myself I would read more, widen my choice of companions, but part of the punishment was to leave me with no books. 'Don't give her any more ammunition,' your grandfather had said. 'A corrupt mind twists everything to its advantage.' I missed reading. I missed school. But most of all I missed him, the boy who was sitting opposite me at the Coffee House—I don't even remember his name. After Khaled paid for our cappuccinos and left, I was so moved I held his hand across the table, not below it as we had been doing before in secret, there where all could see. My eyes were brimming with tears of pure happiness. The boy—I wish I could remember his name, he had such beautiful eyes, I can still see them—was more embarrassed than I. He blushed so sweetly. In my captivity I thought of him, and thinking of him made me stronger. I thought to myself, 'All of this doesn't matter because he and I exist in the same world, with the same rivers and seas and mountains.' The foolish girl I was. 'No matter where he is,'

I told myself, 'and no matter how hard they try to keep us apart they'll never stop us gazing into the selfsame sky, the selfsame moon, and being warmed by the selfsame sun.' It gave me great joy to glimpse one of those eternal objects; the sun, a cloud, the blueness of the sky made me feel victorious over their punishment. But, in the end, it was they who won. My arsenal of literary characters shrank rapidly from then on, even Scheherazade would betray me. Now I am unable to read anything longer than a poem or a newspaper article. Books demand too much trust.

"When they released me, I went to the garden to stretch my eyes and breathe the fresh air. My only protest during that month was not to bathe. My knee-long hair was bound up in a bundle and ignored. My eyes fixed on things in the distance that melted. Being able to stretch my sight was like yawning. A breath of stale air escaped from within my blouse. In the fresh air my stench was stronger. I smelled of boiled potatoes. I wondered how he would smell on the nights I will have to lie beneath him? The impulse to cry was replaced by what I understood as anger, but now know was hate. I felt its sudden and swift grip, warm and dependable, mine. That was what spurred me to talk aloud to myself like a mad girl, revealing my thoughts to my father, who I didn't know was on the other side of the wall, listening. I raised my voice in argument, as if Libya and my family had all appeared before me. 'What do you want her to do?' I said into the wind. 'Die? Disappear off the face of the earth? You forbid her school, lock her away for thirty days and now want to marry her to a complete stranger with a big nose. How fantastic!' I saw him coming toward me with that strange serene smile that preceded every beating, not so much a smile as an expression of pain. His lips strained and affected his eyes, he seemed almost regretful. This time the inevitability of it drained me, I couldn't even get myself to speak, to say 'No,' let alone run. I remained still, sitting under the grapevine-shackled trellising that shaded an area spread with rugs, where we sometimes gathered in the late afternoons to drink tea and roast almonds, listening to your grandmother recite from *A Thousand and One Nights*."

I felt my heart tense in fear for her, wondering if he was going to strike her down again with the sandbag-weight of his hand.

"Discussing the nose of a suitor suggested desire, a suggestion I preferred to die before making in the company of el-haj Muftah, your grandfather."

Mama liked to refer to her relatives by how they were related to me: her father was "your grandfather," her brother "your uncle." It made me feel responsible, as if I was to blame for their actions, and made the fact that they were completely absent from our lives even more peculiar. My grandparents' house was in Benghazi, where the family is from, twelve hours' drive away, where my uncles, Auntie Nora and my countless cousins also lived. I always thought that it was because of the distance they never visited, but I later discovered that it was my father's political involvement that had scared them away. People were sometimes arrested just by association. It had seemed quite normal then, as most things in childhood do, but, thinking back on it now, I realize how isolated we were.

"A good, virtuous, chaste girl," Mama continued, "ought to only be concerned with the character of her suitor, not his nose. A beating, I thought, was now inevitable. But there was something in the way he had prolonged the moment that made me think he relished it. My hate tightened around my heart. Then he sat beside me, wrapped his arm around my shoulders and spoke in a way he had never done before. At that moment his strange smile gained a new meaning. Because it had always accompanied the beatings, I had come to read it as an expression of regret toward something he felt he was obliged to do; that the inevitability of the situation was causing his spirit to stir with the contradiction of love and justice. I never suspected he took pleasure in hitting me. In fact, although I always disagreed with his punishment, I also believed that perhaps due to an ancient failing that kept father and child from ever being reconciled I must endure the receiving of it as he must endure its administering. And so I came to interpret his smile as the smile of a troubled man, torn between desire and duty, between what he would rather do and what he must. In this way I rescued him in my memory. Because I never doubted his love. But now, as he sat beside me, his smile seemed to mean something else. Along with his gentle voice and embrace, it was also there to comfort me. I cried. I cried because his mercy was harsher than his justice; I cried because I understood that I was now the property of another man, that beating me was no longer a privilege he could allow himself. That stifled smile now looked like his farewell.

"'Would I ever sell you?' he said, sitting beside me beneath the entangled grapevine. 'Would I ever give you to a man that didn't deserve you?'

"And that was how I knew it was over. A word had been given and a word had been received, men's words that could never be taken back or exchanged. My eyes were no longer yawning, I could focus well now. I remembered his beatings and felt my back grow taller at the realization that they had forever ended. I looked down at my knee touching his and was amazed at how able and enduring the human body is."

I remembered how my back too had grown taller after the white car stopped following us. Then I thought of Ustath Rashid—I had no idea what Baba was going through—how he must be locked away, his body bruised and dirty. Perhaps he too was now sitting beside one of his interrogators, and they had suddenly, and to Ustath Rashid's utter astonishment, placed an arm around his bruised shoulders, then smiled at him. And perhaps he too looked down at their two neighboring thighs and was amazed at how strong the human body was. I touched the places on my chest where Osama's palm heels had stabbed me, and although they still ached, the pain was duller, felt less crucial.

Outside in the garden the crickets sounded. Out of nowhere a bird broke into song, then, as if embarrassed, realized it was alone and fell silent. After a little while Mama's breathing became deep and long; she had fallen asleep. Her arm, still wrapped around my waist, became slack. I imagined what I would have done to save her. In my fantasy I would tap on the window of the room where she was held captive and help her jump out. We would run away somewhere where no one could find us. And to avoid people's gossip we would pretend to be brother and sister, because I would be nine and she fourteen. I would make sesame sticks and sell them to children, delivering them on my big motorcycle. I would spend the money I made on books for her. And one day she would meet that boy she was with in the Italian Coffee House—perhaps by the seashore, or at a café, or in a line in a bakery—and fall in love with him again. Many times I would drive by on my motorcycle and see them holding hands above a table in a café, big, silent smiles on their faces. And after they had found many reasons to be together and all the books in the world were read, it would be time for me to be born. My imagination turned the tale in my head—I saved her, went away with her, then came back to save her again—until sleep curled itself around me and I sank into it, feeling the dark, warm glow of hope spread itself within me.

17

The following morning I sprang out of bed the moment my eyes opened. I could still feel the warm shadow of Mama's arm wrapped around me. First thing I did was to shower—something I usually had to be asked to do—then I dressed in shorts, T-shirt and sandals. She was already up, sitting with the newspaper spread in front of her on the breakfast table. I kissed her hand and chattered on.

"When are we going for a drive? Let's go to Signor Il Calzoni's."

She placed a finger under the line she was reading and said, "Why don't you go play with your friends, habibi?"

I didn't want to see the boys. I went and played in my workshop up on the roof for a while, then I suddenly felt worried about her. I went to find her. She wasn't in the kitchen, and her bedroom door was closed.

"Mama?"

The silence before she spoke seemed endless.

"Yes," she said.

I didn't know what else to say.

"What do you want?" Her voice wasn't right. My instinct was to go in and stay beside her.

"Have you got the time?"

"The time?" Then I heard her say to herself, "What a question!" She cleared her throat then said, louder than necessary, "It's nine. Go and play."

I went out to the garden again and lay in the shade of the glue tree. The sunlight filtered through the branches and leaves, burning their edges white. I recalled a dream I had had that night. Out of nowhere it returned. Mama was ill again. She was laughing at me because I couldn't walk. When I looked down I saw that I had no legs. She giggled in that crazy way she did when she was ill. I realized then that I had grown wings, wings as long as Mulberry Street. She clapped her hands and laughed so hard her eyes were crying. Remembering the dream gave me an excuse to run to her.

I opened her door without knocking. She was lying in bed, newspaper in hand. "I have just remembered a dream, can you work it out for me?" I only got as far as saying, "You were ill again," before she interrupted.

"Why beckon disaster?"

"I am not. It was a dream."

"Don't let such bad thoughts take hold of you."

I faced the ground. "What are you going to make for lunch?"

"Lunch? It's too early for lunch. Are you hungry?"

"No," I said and left the room.

★

I was walking around the garden when I spotted Sharief talking to Ustath Jafer. I ran to my room, fetched the book from beneath the mattress and ran out. I stood beside them, not wanting to disturb their conversation, but unable to calm my excitement. They both looked at me.

"What do you want?" Ustath Jafer asked.

I shook my head and walked away. I put the book on the pavement in front of our house and sat on it, pretending to be drawing in the sand. Sharief nodded several times while Ustath Jafer spoke, pointing at our house, then at Ustath Rashid's. Then he waved his hand at Sharief as if to say, "Off you go," and walked into the dark shade of his house.

Sharief got into his car. I went to him.

"This is the book I told you about," I said, handing him Baba's book, *Democracy Now*.

He took it, turned it in his hand, then handed it back.

"It's from Ustath Rashid to Baba."

"Umm," he said, uninterested.

"Look," I said, opening the book, pointing to the dedication. He squinted at it. "I have names too." He didn't seem to know or care what I was talking about. "Names to vouch for Baba, remember? I have Rashid," I said, pointing at Ustath Rashid's house. "Nasser. And Moosa."

"Nothing new," he said irritably, reaching for the keys in the ignition. I could see the line where the dry, dark skin of his lower lip ended and the moist, paler flesh on the inside of his mouth began. I looked at the infinite pockmarks etched on his cheek, each a different size and shape, the skin in them shiny and a shade lighter. He turned the engine on. "I wouldn't worry if I were you," he said. "Your father was very cooperative, melted like butter." He motioned toward

Ustath Jafer's house. "And now a mighty hand has come to his rescue." I was leaning against the car. "Move," he said and drove off without saying good-bye.

I stood in the street, unable to make any sense of what Sharief meant by "cooperative," "melted like butter." The sun had nibbled away all the shade, burning our dirt street white. It seemed an effort just to keep my eyes open. I walked into our house, thankful for its cool shade, thankful for the roof above it, blinking to erase the blotches of light stamped into my retina.

★

Later that day Moosa arrived. He was in a very agitated state and seemed unable to settle in one place.

"Tripoli is being turned upside down. They took everyone, gathering them like sheep."

"Where's Faraj?"

"I don't know. Turn on the television. Rashid. Rashid will be judged . . . *Judged?* I mean . . . The bastards."

"When, when?" Mama asked. His restless anxiety had been transmitted to her.

He turned on the television in the sitting room and sat on the sofa. She sat beside him. Every time she tried to speak he raised his hand in the air.

Ustath Rashid was sitting down, a spotlight on his face. The broadcast was a repeat of what I saw during naptime, but now it was evening, the whole world awake to see it. "Were you present at the meeting?" Ustath Rashid hesitated, then nodded and said, "Yes, I was present." Then repeated, "Present, present," loud enough now that there could be no doubt. Then the picture changed, they didn't show him saying, "No," to Baba's name. Instead, a man

now sat at a desk strewn with papers. He sat like a news re-
porter, but from his clothes and his helmet of curly hair I
knew he was a member of the Revolutionary Committee.
"Dark elements," he said in the high, barking tone in which
Revolutionary Committee announcements are usually delivered. "Traitors who despise and envy our revolution have
been detected. We, the Revolutionary Committee, the
Guardians of the Revolution, have captured all members of
this misguided group and those who harbored and funded
them and will punish them severely." The man looked
straight into the camera and added, "The enemy has been
miserably defeated. Long live the Guide, long live the
September Revolution." The camera stayed on him for
longer than was necessary. He eventually called out,
"Enough. I am finished." Then the screen went black for a
few seconds before the flowers came on again, this time accompanied by revolutionary songs.

I was standing in the doorway, the same doorway where
Sharief had stood, Sharief who by now must have returned
to sit in his car outside our house, loyal, eternal, sure of his
place in the world, heavy with a man's odor. I walked into
the room and sat on the floor midway between the sofa
and the television. Neither of them told me to leave. We
watched the pink flowers and listened to the confident songs
of the revolution, when, without explanation, the broadcast
returned. All you could see was the dark night sky and,
at the bottom of the screen, heads burnished by spotlights.
Someone whispered, "Zoom," then irritably, "Zoom, zoom
out." The camera swung down and now all we could see
was the concrete floor. A foot stepped into the picture. I
could see the threadbare stitching on the man's black leather
shoe and the motif of an eagle with its wings outstretched on

the narrow metal buckle that went across the front. "I said zoom out, you idiot. Move." The foot stepped out and the camera moved up and zoomed out.

"They are at the National Basketball Stadium," Moosa said softly to Mama or to himself.

"Which one? Where?"

"The new one on the way to town."

"And what are they doing there?" Mama asked, raising her voice.

Interrogations were always conducted in windowless rooms. Moosa said nothing, and I, fearing Mama would send me away to practice my scales, didn't look back.

The National Basketball Stadium was full. The camera panned the tiers; not one seat was empty. Most of the spectators wore something green: a shirt, an arm- or headband. Who are we playing, I wondered? Basketball wasn't a game I liked, but whenever Libya played against another country, no matter the sport or game, I was riveted, glued to the television screen. Once I sat for six hours watching a close chess match between a Libyan and a Korean at the International Chess Championship in Moscow. When the Korean won I almost cried with disappointment.

The camera finally turned to the court. A long table was positioned at its center. Whoever put it there made sure its middle was exactly on the court's centerline. It was meticulously decorated in the style of a news conference desk: its top neatly covered with a white tablecloth and on its front, hiding the feet of the seated committee, a green fabric fell precisely to the floor. Three people sat at the long table, two men and a woman. A bottle of water and an empty glass stood in front of each one. A microphone was placed in front of the man in the center. He tapped it twice, then began reading from a piece of paper in his hand.

"The consummate revolutionary leader of the world revolution for a new civilization, Muammar el-Qaddafi, the Leader of the Libyan people, the symbol of hope and freedom, the Son of the Desert . . ." He looked up, checking the mood of the crowd, ". . . because," he said, raising his voice, pointing his index finger toward the sky, "because it was in the desert where our Leader was born, in the desert where God spoke to Moses, in the desert where the prophet Elijah heard the still voice of God ordering him to face the tyranny of an oppressive ruler, in the desert where Christ prepared himself through fasting and prayer for a mission that was to shape Western history, in the solitude of the desert where the Prophet Muhammad contemplated the order of creation and the sad state of his own people"—Mama and Moosa didn't, but I said "Peace and blessings be upon him" after each prophet's name—"and it was also in the desert where our Leader, the Guide, the Savior of the Nation, our Great Teacher and Benefactor, the Father of the Great el-Fateh of September Revolution, Muammar el-Qaddafi, was born, lived, dreamed and reflected."

The crowd leaped up, cheering. "Turn, turn," a voice whispered, and the cameraman swung the camera on the happy and clapping spectators. Mama and Moosa were still and quiet. "This purest of hearts . . ." The man tried to continue. He looked down and held his hand in a fist above him and pounded rhythmically at the air. "This . . ." He was unable to break the jubilant howl of the spectators. "This purest . . ." he said in a voice like a high-pitched siren, like Sheikh Mustafa's voice as it crackled with emotion during the Friday sermon. "This purest of hearts, the emblem of single-mindedness, the symbol of courage, dedication and self-determination, our consummate Leader and Benefactor, who teaches us abundantly by example, has prevailed." For a moment he lost his voice. The woman to his right poured him a glass of water. He took a sip and continued. "People, masses, brothers, sisters, today is a day to relish. Today we have defeated the corrupt elements that tried to undermine our achievements and hinder our march." The crowd came in, more jubilant and eager, desperate to express their commitment. Someone tried to say something to the cameraman. He couldn't hear and shouted, "What?" Just then the chaotic cheering merged into a chant, even the cameraman and the one beside him joined in: "El-Fateh, the revolution of the masses! El-Fateh, the republic!" Chaotic shouting reigned again before another chant emerged: "With our blood! With our soul! We'll defend our Guide!" The camera moved, the picture blurred, then focused on one of the basketball nets. It zoomed out quickly onto the backboard, then moved down to where a man, seated on the shoulders of another, was struggling to tie a rope. Then he kicked his heels into the man beneath him and his bearer moved. When they were out of the picture the camera zoomed out a little and showed a rope hanging from behind the backboard, swinging with a loop at its end.

I looked back at the sofa. Both Mama and Moosa sat erect. Moosa's hands fell locked between his knees, and there was a somber grimace on his face, whereas Mama's face was completely blank. I had never seen it like this before. Her face gave absolutely nothing away. I remembered Ustath Rashid once showing Kareem and me a book of very old portraits from Fayoum. They were beautiful, but something was odd about them. Then he told us how they were made. "Because they didn't have cameras in those days," he explained, "when a family lost a loved one they got a painter to do a portrait of the deceased. And because no one likes to remember the dead dead, the painters did their best to make the person look alive. They gave them beautiful rosy cheeks, big round eyes and sometimes even a crown of jasmine or olive leaves." Mama now looked like a Fayoum portrait, still, wide-eyed, beautiful, but lifeless. I recalled Ustath Rashid's peculiar statement: "If you look closely you can see the shadow of death in the picture. They are unique in that each and every one of them is void of desire."

The crowd's chanting and cheering was so loud, so hysterical and constant, that it fused into a continuous hum, like the hum of a giant vacuum cleaner. When the people calmed down, the camera moved on to the court again. A few meters in front of the committee, another man was now present. He had his hands tied behind his back and was sitting cross-legged on the floor in front of a microphone on a stand. He kept looking behind him at the rope.

"There he is," Moosa said.

Then the camera zoomed in and we could see that the handcuffed man sitting on the floor of the National Basketball Stadium was Ustath Rashid. His forehead shone with sweat. His mustache too was moist, tears silvered his cheeks. He didn't cry honorably, he cried like a baby. He looked back at the rope, then at the committee who were to one side of him, and said something inaudible.

"Speak into the microphone," the man in the center ordered.

Ustath Rashid looked to one side and saw a man come from behind. He looked up at him, tried to say something. If

I had to guess what, it would be something like: "I kiss your feet, for God's sake, for your parents' sake," because when the man placed his hand on the microphone to adjust it Ustath Rashid tried to kiss it. When the man walked away Ustath Rashid looked back, searching for him.

"What do you have to say in your defense?" the man at the center of the table said.

Ustath Rashid looked at him and cried again. He checked the hanging rope then turned to the man, raising his eyebrows, pursing his lips, pleading like a guilty child.

"We are giving you a chance to defend yourself. If you are innocent, speak," the man said with a grin, leaning back in his chair and looking to the man and woman on either side of him, who seemed to understand his humor.

"Innocent, innocent . . . Innocent." Ustath Rashid latched on to the word.

"But we have a confession here," the woman on the panel shouted into the microphone. The crowd became excited. The man at the center leaned toward her and seemed to be saying, "Let me handle this." She nodded gravely, straightened her blouse, then suddenly became surprised, pleased, waving at someone in the crowd.

"Are you saying you didn't confess?" the man asked, holding a piece of paper in his hand.

Ustath Rashid shook his head, then nodded, contorting his face again, tilting his head to one side. "I confess, I confess," he repeated, then taking a deep breath he sighed, "I confess," as if under the harshness of the spotlights, sitting on the crisp, multicolored plastic floor of our new National Basketball Stadium, which was designed to the highest international standards, he needed to hear it once more for himself. Then he seemed to wake up. He looked up at the panel.

"Mercy," he said, tilting his head and repeating that word a few times, looking back at the hanging rope before crying again.

The crowd went crazy, as if that one word was the final proof they were all waiting for. A shoe came flying and landed beside him. He looked at it, looked at the crowd and cried, repeating something inaudible now. Maybe he was saying, "Mercy" or "I confess" or "Innocent," or maybe he too had seen someone he recognized, a friendly face.

Two men came from behind him and pulled him up from under his arms. He was still wearing the same white shirt that was too big for him, the one he had been wearing in the televised interrogation. He seemed to be begging the men dragging him toward the hanging rope. He reminded me of the way a shy woman would resist her friends' invitation to dance, pulling her shoulders up to her ears and waving her index finger nervously in front of her mouth. The crowd was jumping now, jumping and howling, *Hang the traitor! Hang the traitor!* When the men stood him below the rope he tried to kiss one of their hands again. His lips were now as thin as licorice sticks when pulled at either end. Someone behind him was motioning eagerly for assistance, then a ladder appeared. It was a wide, sturdy-looking aluminum ladder. It shone under the bright lights. It looked brand-new, feathers of ripped plastic stuck out around its feet. Ustath Rashid was made to climb it. At every rung he stopped and begged for mercy. He was pushed along with a strange tenderness, with a mere nudge to his elbow. But after a couple of times the man nudging him seemed to reach the end of his patience. He climbed up beside him and pulled him up by the arm. Ustath Rashid was now halfway up. The rope brushed against his face, making him blink. The man placed the rope around Ustath Rashid's neck and tightened it. Then he slapped the air beside his ear as if to say, "There, done" or "See how easy?" and climbed down. Ustath Rashid's body sagged a little.

"He's fainting," Moosa said, in the same slow, elongated way in which he had been offering his commentary throughout.

Mama said nothing.

Moosa was right. Ustath Rashid slipped off the ladder and was snatched by the rope. This caused an uproar; the crowd was ready. He was propped up, slapped a couple of times across the face, then turned toward the camera. We could see now that his trousers were wet. Something yellow appeared from his mouth and seemed to grow. No one wiped it off, no one brought him a glass of water, a toothbrush and toothpaste to wash away the burning and greedy acid. His head didn't shake in disgust, he seemed to be oddly comfortable with his vomit.

The camera turned to the spectators. They were punching the air and cheering. Several women ululated. And suddenly, like a wave rising, the cheering became louder and more furious. The camera swung quickly, and we saw Ustath Rashid swinging from the rope, the shiny aluminum ladder a meter or two to one side, too far for his swimming legs. The crowd spilled down on to the court now. Some of the spectators threw their shoes at Ustath Rashid, a couple of men hugged and dangled from his ankles, then waved to others to come and do the same. They looked like children satisfied with a swing they had just made. Everybody seemed happy. I looked back. Moosa's cheeks were silver. I had never seen him cry before. Mama stared blankly at the television. I turned and continued watching. After a few more seconds of chaos the flowers returned, still and pink, with the national anthem playing confidently in the background. When I looked back again Mama and Moosa were gone.

★

I found her sitting at the breakfast table smoking one of Moosa's cigarettes. He was filling a teapot with water. I sat down beside Mama.

"Madness," she said, the cigarette trembling in her hand. The silence that followed seemed to agree with her. "Instead of begging, he should've said something," she added.

Moosa placed the tea on the table.

"Did you see how the crowd reacted?" Mama said.

"Madness," Moosa confirmed.

And in this way they both went over the details of what we had just seen and in their recalling there was comfort. I mentioned his trousers darkening with urine. Mama hadn't noticed this detail, but Moosa had. I was glad when he backed me up on it. She had seen the vomit. That seemed to convince her that we were right about the urine.

"Poor Salma," she said.

"May God compensate her and grant her patience," Moosa said.

"Amen," Mama added.

I thought of saying, "Poor Kareem," but I didn't.

18

That night the rain fell for hours. Swamps covered our street and reflected the house lights. Our roof was a shallow pool of rainwater. I walked in it, relishing the resistance of the water against my bare feet. I lay in bed going over the dark episode, looking for how it could have been different, but I couldn't imagine a happy ending. Shut or open, my eyes continued to see the slim figure of Ustath Rashid swinging in midair, the dark stain of urine expanding around his groin, his ankles shuddering one last time the way sheep kick after slaughter, men hugging his legs, women ululating into the night air.

Mama, too, was unsettled. When at some point in the night I woke up frightened and went to lie beside her, she jolted. "No," she said, her hand against my chest, her voice murky but urgent in the dark. "Go. Sleep in your bed," then, as if checking herself, she added, "habibi."

★

The following morning Mama was gone. A bottomless fear propelled me from room to room searching for her. Then I heard her keys in the front door. She walked in, calling my name.

"You're not dressed yet?" She was all in black, her face bare of makeup, her hair tied in a ball. "Quick. You must come to say good-bye." She was collecting empty plastic bags. "Salma and Kareem are going to Benghazi. She has a brother there, he has come to fetch them, drove all night. Remember to say your commiseration." Then she pointed her index finger and said, "Say: 'May God compensate you and have mercy on Ustath Rashid.'"

I got the same hollow feeling in my belly as on the mornings when we had to take the antiflu shot at school, when we all had to stand in line with one sleeve rolled up to the shoulder, watching those at the front cry with pain. Once I ran away and was chased by two teachers who dragged me to the head of the line: "Do him now so we won't have to chase him again," they said to the nurse. Somehow the prospect of seeing Kareem after what had just happened to his father frightened me just as much. "Grief loves the hollow; all it wants is to hear its own echo," Mama had said.

I followed her in my pajamas and when I had gathered enough courage I said, "I want to stay here."

"Don't you want to say good-bye to Kareem? Poor boy, he looks like he's had a terrible night. His eyes are swollen like two tomatoes."

I didn't know what to say. I imagined his face and imagining it made me want to run to him.

"It's up to you," she finally said. "After all, he's *your* friend." She was busy collecting other things now: napkins, a bottle of water. "But if you want to see him you must hurry, they are loading the car." When I didn't reply she said, "Shall I tell them you are still asleep?" I nodded.

She left and I walked slowly, aimlessly, around our house. I went out to the garden. It was morning, but the sun was as strong as it would be at noon, bleaching everything. I remembered Salah Abd al-Sabur's words: *Noon, you fill my heart with fear and dread, showing me more than I want to see.* The rain puddles had vanished, and in their place the earth was a shade darker. I climbed up to the roof to spy on them. Kareem's garden was empty. All the windows were closed and sealed with curtains. A car stood in front of the house, its sides brushed with sprays of caked dirt. It's a twelve-hour drive to Benghazi. I could see a pair of knees beneath the steering wheel, a man's knees. Then I heard him yell, "Come on!" Mama appeared out of their house, walking hurriedly, carrying the plastic bags she had collected, bulging full now. The man got out of the car, slamming the door hard behind him. "It's unbelievable how long they are taking!" he said, irritably. He opened the trunk for her. "They'll be out soon," Mama said, carefully placing the plastic bags in the car. He must be the uncle Mama mentioned. Mama stood beside him, rubbing her hands together. His fists were visible in his pockets. I wondered how Kareem will get on with him. Then Auntie Salma appeared. She, too, was in black. She hugged Mama and sobbed. Mama patted her back and said, "Patience, dear, patience." The man yelled again, "Kareem, what are you doing in there?" I imagined Kareem walking through his house, maybe smelling his father's pillow one last time. Then he appeared, walking slowly and not paying any attention to his uncle. He opened the car door and sat in the front, in the seat beside the driver. He looked ahead, I could see the side of his face. I felt that at any moment he was going to turn and face me, then they drove away. I watched the dust gather behind them.

★

Mama spent that whole day on the telephone, taking calls from relatives. I answered the first few. "People are gossiping," they said. "Saying that the man yesterday, God forbid, was your neighbor and a good friend of Bu Suleiman. We had hoped it wasn't true."

Then, by early evening, Um Masoud brought over our crystal cake plate full of cookies. "I haven't come empty-handed," she said, smiling mischievously. "And I don't mean the cookies. I bring news." She marched ahead and into the kitchen. The expression on Mama's face was suspended between hope and grief. Then Um Masoud turned toward us, smiling. Mama rushed to her side.

"Settle down, girl, settle down," she said, laughing. "First, make us tea."

And without hesitation Mama switched to the task. I watched Um Masoud sitting at our kitchen table and wondered if this was the way her husband, Ustath Jafer, behaved toward her. She seemed to relish the silence that had to be assumed while Mama made the tea. Mama's hands trembled as she arranged the cups.

"Well," Um Masoud began. "Jafer called and . . ."

"What did he say? Has he found him?"

Um Masoud smiled, and when Mama asked, "Where is he?" she held out her hand and shut her eyes.

"Now I don't have all the facts. But I am sure you'll see him very soon."

Mama began to cry. "Thank you, thank you," she said.

On her way out Um Masoud said, "He might not look well," then, looking at me, "You know how the little ones can get nightmares."

★

She paced up and down the hallway. She washed her arms to the elbow, her feet, put a towel over her head and spread a prayer rug. Her lips mimed the words, she didn't look comfortable sitting on her bent knees. When the telephone rang she ran to it.

"Yes, Um Masoud. Here's his number," she said. "His name is Moosa Yaseen."

Then she called Moosa. "Stay by the telephone. They will call you to fetch Faraj. Call me as soon as you hear anything."

She smoked incessantly even though she wasn't ill. When I said I was hungry she made me a sandwich with a cigarette between her lips. She couldn't be still.

Around ten Moosa called.

"Any news? Why are you calling, then? What if they call now and find the line busy? Hang up."

It was getting late. I could barely keep my eyes open. She put me to bed and when she kissed my forehead she seemed to linger.

★

The following morning she came to my room.

"Good news," she said, pulling the curtain open. The morning light was brilliant and harsh. She opened the window. Birds were busy chanting and seemed too eager. Her face was overtaken with what seemed to be happiness. "Something wonderful has occurred. God has looked into our case." She went around my room, picking up and folding clothes. "We must slaughter a sheep, no, a calf, and invite Jafer and Um Masoud and their two sons. What decent people they are."

The doorbell rang. It didn't ring in Baba's special ring. "Praise be to God," Mama said, then, "You stay here. Don't leave your room." She closed the door behind her. I heard Moosa's voice struggle under a heavy weight. I wondered if he was bringing in another picture of the Guide—perhaps now, I thought, we must hang one in every room. "Wait," Mama whispered. "OK, bring him here." I heard them enter Mama's room and close the door behind them. They remained there for a while. Then I heard one of them leave the room. I went to the kitchen and found Moosa sitting there. He seemed far away, like someone who had just survived an accident. His shirt had dark brown spots on it. When I asked him what they were he said, "Just a bit of blood, that's all." Then after a short silence he added, "I lost a tooth."

I heard Mama go from her room to the bathroom a few times, always closing the bedroom door behind her.

"I will pass by later," Moosa said and left.

I went to Mama's room and knocked.

I thought I heard a man's voice first, then she whispered, "Don't worry, don't worry." The door opened wide enough for her to squeeze through it. "What?"

"Who's in there?"

She took me by the hand to the kitchen. "Now listen, Suleiman. I am going to tell you something very important.

Baba is home. He's a little unwell and so needs peace and quiet."

"Baba is . . . He's . . ." Whatever words I tried to utter shattered in my mouth. But she understood.

"Yes, yes. But he's not feeling well. He's resting. You mustn't disturb him, you mustn't disturb him at all," she said, walking away, back to their room.

★

When I went to use the bathroom I found the mirror above the washbasin covered with a white bedsheet. I lifted one corner and saw nothing different about the mirror.

After a while Mama came to ask, "Where's Moosa? Where did he say he was going? At a time like this we should stay together."

"He said he'll pass by later."

"Did he say when?"

"Later. He just said later."

"At a time like this we should stay together," she repeated.

"Why is the mirror in the bathroom covered?" I asked.

"He knows I need to talk to him. I hate it when he leaves without saying."

"Why did you cover the mirror?"

"Did you remove it?" she said anxiously.

I shook my head.

"Don't touch it."

★

I wasn't allowed to even peek in on Baba.

"In the morning," Mama said, standing between me and the entrance to their room.

The door was left ajar, but everything inside was black. I didn't hear Baba's heavy breathing, nor did the room smell of sleep, but it had the silence of someone in it.

"Baba?" I called.

"In the morning," she repeated, pushing me away. "And don't come to him. If he feels up to it he'll come to see you."

At first I didn't think anything of it, but when I was brushing my teeth I remembered that it was Thursday night, that the next day was Baba's day off, and it puzzled me why Mama didn't want me to wake him up when on Friday mornings I always ran to his bed and pounced on him. It made him sit up startled, blowing air.

★

How could it be so easy? What was absent in the stadium? What didn't intervene to rescue Ustath Rashid? Perhaps it was all the cowboy films with their logic of happy endings that made me think this way, that perhaps it wasn't God but they who had invented hope and the promise that just at the point when the hero had the rope around his neck, suddenly, and with the Majesty of God, a shot would come from nowhere and break the rope. The hero would kick the man beside him, and the rest of the mob—the *cowards*—would jump on their saddles and ride off, up and over the hill. Everyone at the cinema would jump and shout and clap and hug one another as if it was a football match. Tears would come down my face, but it wouldn't matter because many cheeks, grown men too, would shine with tears. I recalled the joy of such moments and how they seemed to burn a hole through my chest. Where were the heroes, the bullets, the scurrying mob, the happy endings that used to send us out of the dark cinema halls rosy-cheeked with joy, slapping one another's backs, rejoicing that our man had won, that God was with him, that God didn't leave him alone in his hour of need, that the world worked in the ways we expected it to work and didn't falter? Something was absent in the stadium, something that could no longer be relied on. Apart from making me lose trust in the assumption that "good things happen to good people," the televised execution of Ustath Rashid would leave another, more lasting impression on me, one that has survived well into my manhood, a kind of quiet panic, as if at any moment the rug could be pulled from beneath my feet. After Ustath Rashid's death I had no illusions that I or Baba or Mama were immune from being burned by the madness that overtook the National Basketball Stadium.

19

At first I thought I had woken up very early because the light from my window sparkled like early-morning light and I couldn't hear anyone in the house. I peed, enjoying the jet of my urine, the crystal froth it created. I went to see what time it was on the big clock in the hallway. Eleven-thirty. I felt a sinking dread at the thought that Mama and Baba had gone out without me. Their door was ajar. Through the gap I saw their forms buried in the sheets. The curtains were open, but the window was shut. I had never known them to sleep this late. I wanted to say, "Wake up, sleepyheads," but I didn't. I thought I could detect a strange smell coming from the room. The large mirror on Mama's dresser was also covered in a white sheet, and her small hand-mirror lay mute on its face. Why this hiding of mirrors, I wondered.

I went to the kitchen and sat at the breakfast table. It was almost noon. Will they ever wake up? What if they had both died in their sleep? I imagined my life without them and in imagining it I felt a flutter of excitement in my belly. Although I didn't understand it, nor ever dared or knew how to confess it, this wasn't unusual; I often fantasized about losing those I loved the most: imagining their funerals, the mourners, me being the remaining solitary orphaned figure in black. I went to see if they were alive.

I entered their bedroom. I was struck by how terrible the smell in there was. It reminded me of the stink of a dog the boys and I had found one day on our way back from school dead with a swarm of flies buzzing around its bloated belly. But then I saw Mama's back rise and fall with breath. Baba lay beside her entirely covered in the bed sheet.

I sat at the breakfast table again. After a few minutes I heard one of them enter the bathroom, then the flush of the toilet and the hiss of the cistern. When I heard the bathroom door open I lifted the chair beside me and let it drop. I hoped it was Baba. But Mama walked in squinting against the light. "Good morning," she said, opening the fridge, yawning. She pressed a bottle of water against her lips and I watched the liquid fatten her throat with every gulp. She took a big breath and, looking up into the ceiling, said, "We survived the madness."

"Is Baba still asleep?"

She nodded and kissed me on the head. I didn't kiss her hand. She filled the teapot with water and clicked the spark several times before the burner caught fire.

"He's very tired," she said, yawning. "We both sat up talking most of the night, slept just after it was light."

"What did you talk about?"

"Nothing."

"Where was he?"

"On business."

I felt my throat tighten with anger.

"When will he wake up?"

"He'll wake up when he wakes up."

I felt a rush of things come tumbling in my head before I heard myself scream, "When will he wake up?" Then all the breath left me, sucked out by a world that had no air in it. I was shut out, my nails clawed at the wooden surface of the table.

"What's the matter? Calm down. Breathe. Look at me, look at me. That's it. Keep your eyes here. It's over. You're OK now. Breathe, habibi, breathe."

She poured a glass of water and insisted I drink it.

"You always lie. I am not a child and you always lie." When I looked at her she wasn't angry. She looked worried and tender. "Don't ever ask me to practice my scales again. They killed Ustath Rashid. Is Baba dead too?" She looked astonished by my question. "Is that why I am not allowed to see him? Has he begun to rot, is that why your room stinks?"

"No. No." Then she sighed and said, "Wait here, I'll be back."

After a short time I heard her call, "Slooma, come, your father wants you."

I went to her and stood at the entrance. I was immediately unsettled because the curtains were now drawn across and it was as dark as night in there. The stink of death was unbearable.

"Come in," she said.

Entering the room felt like entering the sea. The only light came in from behind me and fell on the floor.

"Close the door behind you," she said.

The darkness thickened. The mighty French velvet curtains kept the daylight out. "Where are you?" I asked.

"We are here," she said.

Baba, if he was there, if he was alive, was as quiet as stone.

"Where's Baba?" I wanted to switch on the light.

"I am here," he said. His voice startled me. It was thick, deep and distorted by teeth and a blocked nose. But the scariest thing was that I could recognize him in it. It was Baba, Baba after he was no longer Baba, maybe even, I thought from within my fear and confusion, Baba after he ceased to be alive.

"Why can't I see him?" I asked, fear urging me to switch on the light or pull open the thick curtains.

"You can, habibi," he said, "but not now. Maybe tomorrow," a wire of grief tearing at his voice.

"Why not now?"

"Because Baba has got a terrible headache and light bothers him," Mama said quickly. I knew she was lying.

"Where did you go, Baba?"

"Don't pester your father with endless questions," Mama said. "I told you he has a headache."

After a few silent seconds in the dark, Mama's cool, open palms fell on my eyes and lips. She turned me around and pushed me out.

She took me to the kitchen and said, "See? Your father is fine." She placed a hand on my cheek, "Go now, play in the garden, habibi," and smiled as if I had done something good, as if I had just finished playing for her guests one of her favorite songs on the piano, something by Abd al-Wahab or Fareed al-Atrash.

★

The noon sun was vertical. As soon as it fell on my head I felt its pressure. Doubt that the man in Baba's bed was Baba also pressed on me, and I felt unable to escape it.

"But of course he's Baba."

"How do you know?"

"Because he's in there and your mother says so."

"But you know how she lies."

"Don't say that. She keeps truths and she does it only for your own good."

I walked under the trees in the shade, around the house. When I reached their bedroom window I saw the curtains open. "But I thought the light bothered him," I heard myself say. I couldn't see in because of the reflection on the glass. I came closer, cupped my hands around my eyes and saw a naked man sitting on the bed, his back criss-crossed in dark glistening lines, some oozing blood. Suddenly he turned toward me. His horrible face threw me back. I fell beneath the glue tree. His eyes were closed, full of air or water or blood, like split rotten tomatoes, and his lower lip was as fat and purple as a baby eggplant. I heard him shout in his horrible, bubbling voice, "Najwa, Najwa, draw the curtains." Mama appeared at the window. She watched me for a moment—my heart was pounding, I was still on the ground, gasping for breath—then with one stroke she pulled the curtains shut.

"You see?" I whispered to myself. "He's not Baba." I ran into the house. I was standing in front of their bedroom door. I knocked. "Who's in there?" I screamed, my voice full of fear. They didn't answer. "If you don't answer I swear I'll open the door," I said and pushed the door open.

I ran to the curtains and pulled them open. The naked

monster was under the covers again, pretending to be asleep, pretending to be Baba. And Mama was sitting on the bed beside it, looking at me. She seemed almost frightened. I wanted to tell her, "Don't worry, everything will be all right." I opened the window instead. Somehow I felt we, Mama and I, would be safer this way. The new air seemed to wash the room.

"Baba doesn't want you to see him like this," Mama said.

Suddenly the figure under the sheets sat up on the edge of the bed, giving me its back, wrapping its body in the white bed sheet that was stained with thin lines of blood. Slowly I began to recognize him: his wavy black hair, the modest hills of his shoulders, the neck I massaged many times and many more times buried my face in to kiss and make the ticklish sound of a fart that always made him laugh. Tears choked me.

"Baba?" I tried to say.

He twitched. "Take him away. Please."

"It's no good now. He saw you."

"Baba?"

"Yes," he snapped, as if the effort to speak was punishing him. "Take him away, he'll get nightmares."

"I almost never get nightmares."

After a few seconds, during which I thought I must leave or else the world wouldn't continue, Baba spoke. "My eyes aren't working properly. I am . . . ill." Then he shook his head and waved his hand behind his back. I thought of running to kiss it a thousand and one times. "Najwa," he said, the gesture of his hand finally making sense, "please, take him away."

20

Later that day Moosa arrived. Where has he been, Mama asked, and why didn't he say something before leaving? He thought she and Baba needed to be alone after such a traumatic experience, he explained.

"You told Suleiman you'd be passing by later, don't say you'll be passing by later when you have no intention of doing so. The last thing I need now is to worry about you."

"How are you, Champ?" Moosa asked me, his weak smile full of effort.

"There's a monster in our house," I thought of telling him. But he seemed elsewhere. His eyes darted around the room, and then he walked off toward the bathroom. Mama and I followed him. He bent over the basin and began to wash his hands. "How's Bu Suleiman?"

"Thankfully all of his wounds are on the surface," Mama said. "They broke one rib, but nothing else. He just looks . . ." She shook her head and sighed deeply. I, for some reason, did the same. I remembered how Siham had copied her old father's gesture. Moosa noticed the bedsheet covering the mirror above the basin. "He made me cover the mirrors. He doesn't want to see himself. He doesn't want Slooma to see him either," she said, running her fingers through my hair as if she and I had discussed all of this before, shared all the details and retold them to each other so many times neither of us could truly say who had first told the story to the other.

Moosa was no longer wearing the bloodstained shirt he had on the day before, but he still seemed keen on cleaning himself, as if he had just returned from a long drive through the desert. He turned down his shirt collar, baring his thick long neck. He soaped his face and beard, his ears and neck, then splashed cold water on them. Mama and I took a step back to avoid getting wet. He dried himself vigorously, then pulled out a comb from his back pocket, puffed out his cheeks and combed his beard. When he had finished he looked at us for a moment, then walked out. He knocked twice on Baba's door. "Bu Suleiman?" he called and opened the door just wide enough to enter, then shut it behind him. Mama and I stood outside. We heard everything Moosa said, he was speaking loudly as if Baba was deaf.

"How are you?" he asked. Mama placed her ear against the door. "Thank God for your safety. You do look much better than yesterday. You'll be back to normal in no time." Then Baba must have asked him a question. "Don't worry. They are all well. Everyone understands, no one blames you, you had to do what you had to do." Then, after a pause, Moosa asked, "Shall I bring you a glass of water?" and the door opened. Mama was startled. Moosa looked at her for a moment, then squeezed through the door and shut it behind

him. We followed him into the kitchen. He filled a glass of
water and gulped it down. "Does he know about Rashid?"

. "I don't know," Mama said. "I didn't tell him."

He rinsed the glass, filled it and walked back to Baba, but
just outside the kitchen, as if he had heard a balloon explode
in a nearby room, he paused for a second, then continued. I
heard him knock twice and say, in the same loud and opti-
mistic tone, "Bu Suleiman?"

In all of this time Moosa didn't look into my eyes long
enough for me to tell him or ask him anything. His movements were mechanical. I yearned to describe to him, second
by second, what we had watched together on television. I remembered how there was comfort in the retelling of it when
he and Mama and I sat around the breakfast table immediately afterward. There were many details we had neglected,
details I had noticed and was now wondering if he, too, had
seen, like that dark patch of urine that Mama had missed.
There was the way Ustath Rashid had been nudged tenderly
up the ladder, with a mere touch on the elbow, and the sudden frustration at Ustath Rashid's reluctance that had overtaken the man at the bottom of the ladder. I couldn't wait, I
couldn't wait for us to tell it back and forth, over and over,
the way we described scenes in films we liked. And the man
who was walking across the National Basketball Stadium,
in the middle of the chaos, walking calmly from one corner
of the screen to the other, holding a battered black typewriter under one arm as if it was a puppy; did either of them
notice this? I longed to ask Moosa where he thought this
man was going, what he was going to do with a broken
typewriter, and why then and there? It hadn't occurred to
me then that it might be Nasser's typewriter, evidence rescued from the chase.

Mama filled a teapot with water and placed it on a burner. She was moving with certainty now that Baba was home. When she looked over at me and saw that I was looking at her, she smiled, came and kissed me on the cheek. Even though she looked tired, her face was rosy and her eyes sparkled. "It was a narrow escape; now I must focus on you." I had no idea what she meant, but found myself smiling back at her.

We heard someone enter the bathroom and lock the door. After a few minutes Moosa appeared, walking toward the kitchen, clutching the white sheet in one hand. He flung it to one side. "Let him see himself for what he really is," he said; his lower lip was trembling and tears pooled in his eyes. He turned around himself, then left the room. Mama looked at me as if I would know why Moosa was behaving in this way. She followed him, then I heard their voices in the reception room. I stood outside the entrance.

"I can't bear looking at him," Moosa said. "The betrayal in his eyes—I am sorry, I am sorry—his voice scorches me, this is worse than death—forgive me—this is the blackest day of my life."

After a long silence Mama said, "Only yesterday you were ready to die for him, now you wish he had died for you."

"I've been up for two days . . ."

I felt a presence behind me in the hallway. I turned around but found no one there. The walls long and lined with the same infinite bird plucking at the same infinite twig, the swing doors silently shut at the end, the clock ticking monotonously like two people arguing.

"They killed the students closest to us. Rashid is dead, whereas Bu Suleiman is . . . People are talking, saying terrible things about him."

"Let them talk. They would have been first to give him up if it was the other way around."

"Rashid didn't, he didn't. And his wife, the poor woman, now suffers the consequences."

"May God compensate her."

"I don't know how to answer them, I don't know what to say."

"Go home," Mama said suddenly. "It's time you returned to your country."

"This is my country. I've lived here half of my life."

"The only reason you are still alive is because it's not your country."

"There was so much hope, so much hope. Three years ago eight thousand students in Benghazi and four in Tripoli. Twelve thousand students took a stand in an illiterate country of less than three million. We didn't succeed then. It took three years for hope to be reborn, only to see the few who dared sacrificed for the many. One of them, my friend, Muhammed . . ." he said and wept.

Mama's voice too now was tearful. "Stop, Moosa, please. Praise the Prophet."

"He was asking for news, if I knew where Bu Suleiman and Rashid were. I didn't have the heart to tell him. He was calling from inside, barricaded with the others in the university. I didn't have the heart to tell him what was happening outside." Then, in an agitated voice, as if he was blaming Mama, he said, "They gave their lives for their country."

After a long silence Mama said, "They weren't standing for me. May God have mercy on their souls and compensate their families, but they weren't standing for me." Then in a pleading tone she added, "If you want to help us, pack your bags and go home to your family in Cairo."

He sighed. "We have been issued with a deportation notice."

"When must you leave?"

"Tomorrow. Father is furious. He left today."

Again I felt a presence behind me, this time accompanied by a muffled, exhausted breath. Before I could turn, a hand took me by the shoulder and buried me in loose fabric. I immediately wrapped my arms around Baba's waist and I was swallowed up in that stench again. I squeezed and he flinched. He mumbled something I couldn't make out. Then I realized it was my name. When I tried to pull myself away, to see his face, he squeezed me tighter. Mama and Moosa came to see what the noise was. Baba loosened his grip a little and I was able to look up at him. His eyes and lip had grown bigger, redder and bluer. Other details I hadn't noticed before were now visible and in a way they were more disturbing. His left eye was completely shut, but his right eye, close to the nose bridge, was open and as red as blood. A net of small purple veins mapped areas of his cheeks and chin. On one of his temples there was a small burn, a yellow and red circle. I couldn't see the other side of his face but imagined another one there to match it. His jallabia was unbuttoned at the chest, and the same wirelike hairs that I had once pulled sprouted out unharmed.

"What are you doing out of bed?" Mama asked.

"This is still my house, isn't it?" His lower lip, swollen and purple, quivered and distorted his words.

"Come and sit down," she said, pointing toward the reception room.

But he walked away. I walked beside him, my arm wrapped around his waist. The clock's ticking was much livelier than our pace. I let go of him and ran to the clock. I opened its glass door and held the pendulum still. He was in the same place I had left him, favoring one side. I ran to him and when I embraced him he flinched again, tightening his arm around me. When we passed through the hallway swing doors, he stopped for a moment, as if relieved we were alone now. Then he said, quietly like a secret, "Let's go to the garden."

The sun was an hour or two from setting and its light was soft and orange.

"Take me up to your roof."

It's your roof too, I thought. It's our roof. And even though I was holding him and we walked together side by side I felt so far away from him. I squeezed him a little tighter and looked up at his battered face in the warm and dying sunlight.

I waited until he had both feet on the first step before taking the next. And I don't know why at one of our pauses I said, "One by one we'll get there," and immediately hoped he wouldn't respond because anything he would have said would have made me feel awkward.

Life could have spent itself while we climbed those stairs, and I wouldn't have minded.

The roof reminded me of when we burned his books. "We'll buy you new books, Baba." *Democracy Now* was still beneath my mattress. When we reached the top, I slid from beneath his arm, placed his hands on the fence and ran to fetch it. When I returned my heart was beating so fast I could barely speak. "Here," I said and, wrapping his hands around the book, whispered, "I saved this one. Don't tell Mama or Moosa." He held it with one hand to his chest, leaned with the other on my shoulders and we watched the sea. Baba craned his neck. Then I heard his breathing change. "I can hardly see it," he mumbled.

"The sea is quiet today," I said, hoping to distract him. "A good day for swimming, Baba. A good day for lying on your back and floating."

Light shimmered fast on the water like seagulls crowding around food that the jealous sea was keeping from them. He tried to look toward Ustath Rashid's house, but was aiming too high. "Maybe we'll go swimming," I said, and again the hope that he wouldn't respond returned. Then he turned, and I turned with him, like "two halves of the same soul, two open pages of the same book." "Let's walk under the trees," he said.

We went down and walked on the patterns the low sun threw beneath us. I saw the ladder leaning against the wall where I had left it after eating the mulberries. I let go of Baba and climbed the ladder. When I was halfway up I looked down and saw him resting against the wall, holding his rib. I began hunting for mulberries. I altered my eyes to look only for small dark creatures. I walked on my hands and knees along the high wall, negotiating branches, until I found a crown of berries, ripe, red-black with juice and each as big as a beetle. He was sitting on the ground, leaning his back against the wall, holding a small stone—a stone very much like the ones I had thrown at Bahloul, and which on landing on his back had delivered a very satisfying blow— stabbing it into the dirt beside him. When I reached the ground I showed him the berries in my cupped hands and said, "Mulberries, Baba, mulberries. The angels stole them from Heaven to make life easier for us. They are the sweet- est thing." I took one and stuffed it through his swollen lips.

When he didn't move I said, "Chew." He moved his lower jaw up and down a few times then spat it out into his hand. I couldn't understand. I ate one and it was as delicious as ever. "You don't like them?" I said. His deformed lips made him look disgusted. He threw his chewed up berry into the dirt, wiped his hand on his jallabia and, pointing his finger at the small round burn on his temple, said, "They put out their cigarettes here," sucking in air. I looked down at the mulberries in my hands.

21

Baba remained mostly in his room for the following two weeks. Then one morning I woke up to hear him and Mama laughing. They were normal, as if nothing had happened, their voices light, floating with love in our house. Then I heard her sing absentmindedly to herself, the way she used to do when taking a bath or hanging clothes out to dry or painting her eyes in front of the mirror or drawing in the garden. That singing that always evoked a girl unaware of herself, walking home from school, brushing her fingers against the wall, a moment before the Italian Coffee House, before Baba and me and this life. Hearing it unsettled me. It had been a long time since I had heard her sing like this.

After a little while my door swung open and Baba walked in. I pretended to be asleep. My heart raced, thumping below my ears. I felt him sit beside me on the bed. "Slooma," he said gently, his voice improved, almost normal now. When I didn't react he stood up and left the room. I then heard Mama's voice rise and fall in the kitchen.

After holding myself prisoner in my room for a few minutes I got up and went to the bathroom. When I came out, I didn't know which way to go: to the kitchen, where I could hear their voices and the sound of cutlery scraping plates, or back to my room to sleep some more— Maybe I could sleep the whole day through, I thought.

"Slooma," Mama called cheerfully.

They were both sitting at the breakfast table. Baba had a smile on his face. I immediately wanted to ask him why he was smiling, but didn't. He opened his arms and said, "Come, Slooma." His hair was combed and he smelled of cologne. He must have bathed; the wounds on his back must have healed enough for him to bathe.

"Thank God, Slooma," Mama said. "Baba is feeling much better today."

I thanked God out loud to show how pleased I was. He released me from his embrace and held my face in his hands. His hands were trembling, his eyes almost normal. I looked into them, but it was hard to find him there.

After breakfast Mama took to reading the newspaper to him. She read only the international news and whenever the name of our country or leader was mentioned she mumbled it quickly. When he caught me watching him, he smiled.

"I think I will draw today," Mama said, folding the newspaper.

Baba looked at me. I began to feel nervous, nervous in the way you feel when alone in an elevator with a stranger.

"What are you going to do today, Suleiman?" he asked.

I shrugged my shoulders.

Mama returned, clutching pencils in one hand. There was a bowl of fruit in the center of the table. She held each fruit, turning it in her hand, then decided on an orange. She went out into the garden, saying, "I'll be back for a chair and a little table. Yes, I'll need a little table. Oh, I am so excited."

Baba and I were alone again. Just as he took a breath to speak, the doorbell rang.

I ran to answer it. It was Ustath Jafer.

"Hello," I heard Baba say from behind me.

They shook hands. This was the first time Ustath Jafer had ever visited us.

"I am glad to see you up and about."

Baba led him into the reception room, not smiling but blushing slightly. When he turned on the light he did a double take at the large photograph of the Guide. "I am grateful for your help," he said, almost absentmindedly. He turned to me. "Tell your mother to prepare some tea."

I found Mama setting up her table and chair in the garden.

"Ustath Jafer is here."

Her face lit up.

"Baba wants you to make tea."

"But of course," she said, walking briskly to the kitchen.

I went to my room. I felt the need to hear the world. I took my radio and lay with it in bed.

Revolutionary forces [it was the Guide's voice] are capable of and have the right to use terror to eliminate anyone who stands against the revolution. Now we can truly end the old Libyan society and build the new one, where the revolutionary elements help each other in fighting any antirevolutionary movements in the universities, in the factories and in the streets.

Then came the cheers of the crowd, unstoppable, so loud they turned into a wave of noise, drowning everything, and because it became everything and was senseless I longed for the voice of the Guide to return. I went around the dial a couple of times, but every time I returned I found the massive and empty noise of the crowd.

I decided to go for a swim. I put on my swimming shorts, grabbed my flippers and ran out of the house. Mama was back in the garden, drawing her orange, singing to herself. She saw me in my swimming shorts, my flippers beneath my arm.

"Look first," she said, holding a pencil drawing of the orange, double the size of the real one.

"Bye," I said and left.

"When you return I'll have another one. Perhaps with the skin peeled and resting beside it. I remember seeing a painting like that by some European artist. They are very interested in fruit, those Europeans. I wonder why," she mused, looking at her drawing.

★

The ground was hot. I thought of returning to collect my sandals. It was a good walk still to the sea. But to stop the momentum of my steps seemed to require more effort than to keep on moving. I thought of putting on my flippers, but that would have made me walk as slowly and awkwardly as a pigeon. I tried to keep as close as I could to the walls of the houses, but the sun was vertical, the shade narrow and mean. It was quicker to walk in the sun. I walked like an insect, my elbows raised up to my ears, my back arched, my feet curling against the heat. I hopped quickly as if I were dying to pee. Several times I stopped to sit down and give my feet a break, rubbing them and blowing at them. I thought of the bridge sizzling above the fires of Hell, the one we all have to cross to reach Paradise. I held the sea as my target, my paradise. When I reached Gergarish Street, the wide street that follows the shoreline to downtown, I could see heat rippling up from the tarmac. I ran across it, I ran across the sand too and didn't stop until I reached the water-soaked flat sands of the shore. My feet finally in blissful relief. Low wavelets curled their white foamy edges across the turquoise face of the water, the wind was almost still. I looked at the dry sand behind me and wondered how I would walk back.

At the end of the pier, where the waters were as clear as glass, someone was sitting, dangling their feet in the water. For a moment, before I remembered that he and his mother had moved to Benghazi, I hoped it was Kareem. When I got closer and realized that it was Bahloul, I almost laughed. He seemed to be daydreaming. I never imagined Bahloul sitting like this in solitary contemplation. The pier creaked beneath my feet. When I reached him I couldn't help but chuckle, and he turned around, his face disfigured with fear. He seemed to be trembling. This reaction irritated me. I pounded my feet on the wood of the pier and growled—"Grrr"—at him and was reminded of that secret rush of power I had felt chasing him around our garden, throwing stones at his back, hearing my shots land with a satisfying thud, the thumps that made him scream hideously like a horse. He stood up, seeming to consider his escape. How could he be trapped with all of that sea behind him? I made as if to charge at him. He turned solemnly toward the sea and after a short pause jumped into the water. There was something exaggerated about his fall, as if he was jumping from a great height. And only then did I understand why Bahloul hadn't got his boat wet; why, although he had saved up and bought the boat, he hadn't started fishing yet. Bahloul couldn't swim.

I heard his violent and useless splashes. I let go of my flippers and rushed to the end of the pier. I extended my hand to him. I wanted to save him—and he knew it too—he tried to slap his way toward me. He was swallowing water. His jallabia ballooned around him and hindered his efforts. I remembered Mama's warning about diving in to save a drowning person. "Never do it," she said. "A drowning person is so hungry for life they can easily take you down with them." I reached as far as I could, but Bahloul was sinking. When I gave up trying to save him a surge of power came over him. He kicked and slapped the water until he managed to grab hold of one of the pier's legs. I extended my hand but he spat at it, looking around as if expecting someone else to save him. But there was no one, no one but me. Without deciding to I found myself pushing him down with my foot. His knotted hair felt coarse and soggy. He tried to defend himself by grabbing my ankle. This angered me even more. In trying to release my ankle I kicked him in the face. Blood gushed out of his nose into the water. Salty seawater is good for a wound, I knew this well. He began to scream that horse-like scream of his, louder than ever now. I pushed him down again to silence him. Suddenly, without warning, his resistance sank away. I pulled my leg out of the water. After a silence that seemed to last forever, Bahloul sprang up again, coughing and vomiting, dirtying the clear water. He took hold of the pier's column again. He looked at me with a mixture of fear and outrage.

"How's your nose?" I asked.

But he didn't speak, hugging the column and keeping it between us.

I thought of saying sorry, but I collected my flippers and walked away. My heart had never ached with more longing, longing for my true friend, twelve hours away now in Benghazi.

22

The days that followed seemed muffled by dread. Anything that was said in them seemed meaningless and empty. I often felt a quiet anger rise in me, and heard the door slam behind me when I only meant to close it. The first few times this happened I went to where Mama and Baba were and looked at them, expecting one of them to tell me off, but neither did. When I helped Mama set the dining table, I let the plates fall loudly. And I often threw my shoe at the wall when its lace refused to become untangled. I sensed a silent, nervous wave ripple around these sudden outbursts, making me feel that my influence in this world might not be as insignificant as I had thought. And sometimes, when I was in the bathroom and had flushed the toilet, I heard, in the hiss of the cistern filling up, Mama's voice calling me. The first few times this happened I would walk out in an anxious hurry, yelling, "Mama?" the silence seeming endless before I got her voice asking, "Yes, is anything the matter?"

Moosa didn't visit. Once he called, the line crackling. "Slooma," I heard him say then, "where's Mama?" It wasn't like him to be so brief. Mama rushed to the telephone, then snapped her fingers and pointed at the pen and pad. I handed them to her. She wrote something down quickly, asking, "Is it a good school? Are you sure?" Then they were cut off.

★

One exceptionally warm night I woke up from a bad dream. There was no story, just a deep trembling dread hot in my chest. I saw a soft light coming from the sitting room. I couldn't hear Baba snoring. Mama was spread on the sofa, the covers were off, the window beside her wide open. A cricket outside was piercing the night. There was no room to lie beside her. I stood for a moment, considering my options, then I lay on top of her. I hugged her. She woke up with a sudden jolt. "In the name of God," she mumbled quickly, her hand against her chest, her eyes squinting at me. "Suleiman? What are you doing here? Did you have a bad dream?" She took me by the hand back to my room, turned on the bedside lamp, kissed me on the forehead and left.

★

She never fell ill. She never came to my bed to whisper her secret stories of the past. She seemed quite happy with Baba. Some mornings I even heard them giggle together, but when they saw me they stopped. Their new life together, where Baba never went away and Mama was never ill, distanced me from them, and I began, for the first time ever, to long for the summer to end and for school to begin.

One night I was awakened by the sound of a strange moan. I went to their room and saw Baba on top of her again. But this time it was different. Mama didn't lie beneath helpless, her face turned away, with one hand secretly stretched beside her and open toward the sky. Her eyes were glued to his and her legs curled around him, and the moan wasn't his alone; they both shared the pain, it seemed. I didn't wonder this time whether I should intervene. Nothing, it seemed, could stop them. I wanted to take a step further into the room. Maybe if they see me they will stop, I wondered. I wanted them to stop, or pause for a moment.

I ran out through the kitchen, slamming the door behind me, and up to the roof, hiding where my workshop was. The sky was full of stars, I saw them blur beyond my tears, but there was no moon. I am safe, I thought, they wouldn't be able to see me even if they came up here. I waited, breathing as quietly as I could, hugging my knees and the salty smell of their skin. I recalled Sheikh Mustafa's words: "These bodies are our vehicle, they will perish while we will continue." I expected Baba, half naked, his waist wrapped in a towel, to climb up to the roof, angrily calling out my name, followed by Mama, begging him not to hurt me. But no one came. I dried my face and went back. Suddenly the darkness frightened me, and I ran, ran expecting a hand to reach out and grab me around the neck. I sneaked into the kitchen and tiptoed to my room. Their light was still on, they were awake, talking, discussing something in whispers that Mama in particular was barely able to keep down, not angry, but urgent, excited almost. I slammed my bedroom door behind me.

After a few minutes Mama came in and watched me in the faint light that came from their room. I looked straight back at her, not pretending to be asleep, not pretending anything. She closed the door behind her and went back to Baba. I heard them resume their whispered conversation.

★

The following morning I felt Mama's weight sink beside me on the bed, then her fingers in my hair. "You are going on a trip," she said, "to Cairo, to visit Moosa and his family and see the Pyramids."

"But Moosa is here," I said, my voice made older by sleep.

"He left a couple of weeks ago. He said to tell you he can't wait to see you in Cairo."

I turned away from her.

"What's the matter, don't you want to see the Pyramids? They are much bigger than Lepcis."

"I don't want to go," I cried.

Baba came and hugged me. "Come, Slooma," he said.

"Many people would die to see the Pyramids," Mama said.

"I don't want the Pyramids."

"You always wanted to fly though, didn't you?" Baba said.

I nodded. "But school starts soon."

They both looked at each other and, as if considering carefully what he was going to say, Baba said, "You will love Cairo," his voice cut by grief.

23

They drove me to the airport, arguing about which way to go: Baba wanting to take the direct route, Mama insisting we go via Martyrs' Square. There was something she wanted to buy from there, she said. I was made to sit beside him, she sat in the back. The only time we had sat like this was four years before, when I was five, when they had driven me back from the hospital. I had been wearing a white jallabia, the part in front of my groin stained blue-red with iodine. I kept my legs open to relieve the pain, sitting in the front, where there was more leg room, Mama behind, clapping, singing the usual songs. I remembered how I trembled from the shock, from the violation.

Martyrs' Square was thick with people. The sun as wide as the world. Baba parked beside the square.

"I won't be a minute," Mama said, crossed the square and disappeared.

Baba's hands were clutched around the steering wheel.

He had turned the engine off, but the turn signal was still ticking. He stared blankly ahead.

I watched the square, thinking about Nasser. I recalled what his father had said in our house: "People told me they saw a young man run across the square with a typewriter under his arm, chased by a group of Revolutionary Committee men." I pictured him with his typewriter, black and shiny, the same one he had under his arm when I spotted him following Baba into their "headquarters," their secret location on the square, running barefoot, his eyes wide open with fear, his shirt full of air, for a moment hesitating— "This way? No, that?"—before turning into the market, hoping to vanish amid the crowds, when one of his pursuers catches him by the shirt, causing him to turn so fast and the typewriter to fly to one side, the same typewriter on which he had tried, at Baba's request, to teach me how to type, his hands above his head now in anticipation, like Ustath Rashid just before he was kicked in the behind—I think now that perhaps anticipation is the root, the source, of all misfortune—screaming like a horse, the way Bahloul the beggar had done, falling to the ground, the rest of his pursuers catching up with him, kicking him with authority, he is yelling now, calling out for his father to come and rescue him because it was all too much too soon, begging, crying, at one moment his face becomes visible through the forest of legs, a line of blood above one eye, the lower lip as fat as a baby eggplant like Baba's was. Why did we have so much respect for the sight of blood? Why is the sun so unforgiving? "Where is Nasser?" I asked out loud. Baba seemed to wake up from his thoughts. "Where is Nasser?" I yelled at him. "Did they kill him too?" He stared at me, his eyes frightened. I thought of clapping my hands in front of him, but in-

stead dived into him. His body yielded. He held me, folded
on to me. I remembered Ustath Rashid holding Kareem like
this on the bus back from Lepcis, beautiful Lepcis. "I don't
want to leave, I don't want to see the Pyramids," I tried to
say, but my voice was muffled by his clothes.

Then I heard the back door open, Mama's weight nudge
the car. She waited in silence, not asking, "What's the matter, what's the matter?" Then she said, "Let's go," and with
that Baba and I came apart. He turned on the engine. It was
a pleasant sound, a regular, comforting hum governed by
tempered revolutions. He flicked the turn signal in the opposite direction and pulled out. As he took the straight road
it flicked obediently off. I looked back at Mama, she had a
bag full of sesame sticks in her lap, sunglasses covering her
eyes.

★

The airport was empty. I felt as nervous as I had on the first
day of school. Orange plastic chairs lined up in rows like
Boy Scouts across the dark marbled floor. I only noticed she
didn't have a bag with her when Baba was lifting my heavy
suitcase on to the check-in conveyor belt and I remembered
that she had said, "You are going on a trip." "You," not
"we." I told myself off for not noticing this detail before, before when I could have clung to the door frame, the garden
gate, could have run to the sea.

Baba was now busy talking to a woman dressed in a uniform. She had a brooch in the form of a wing fastened to her
lapel. He pointed his finger at her, then placed money in her
hand. She nodded, touched him on the arm and walked
away, smiling the whole time. Then he dug his hands under
my arms and lifted me into his embrace.

"We will come and see you," he said, squeezing me too tightly.

Mama, standing behind him, had one hand over her mouth, her eyes concealed behind the black sunglasses. "You'll be home soon," she said, nodding as if to reassure herself.

"Please don't cry, Slooma," Baba said.

Then I was taken by the stewardess, who seemed to know everything. I looked back and saw Mama in Baba's arms. There they were, the two people I loved the most, the two people I was certain would do anything to keep the truth from me, huddled together in the empty airport, disappearing. Is this the time to wave? But I could no longer see them. In every direction I turned they weren't there.

The truth couldn't be kept away, it was cunning, sly-natured, seeping through at its own indifferent pace, only astonishing in how familiar, how known it has always been. I had known I was going to be sent alone to Cairo, that the name she had written down, telephone receiver held between ear and shoulder, was of my future school, knew it before I noticed she had not brought a bag to the airport, knew it when I cried, "I don't want to leave, I don't want to see the Pyramids," into Baba's belly while Mama was buying the sesame sticks meant to sweeten my mouth, cover the bitter taste, cheat me out of my grief. I knew it and didn't run to the sea. And when I was finally brought to my seat inside the airplane, the airplane I had up to that moment fantasized about entering with my father, both men, both dressed in suits, busy with the world, heavy as all men are, I knew that I would never see my father again, that he would die while I was installed alone in a foreign country to thrive away from the madness.

★

The boom and thunder of the plane taking off frightened me before I looked around and saw how calm all the other passengers were. The hostess who had taken me from Mama and brought me to my seat, into whose delicate hand Baba had stuffed a bundle of tightly folded dinars, kept smiling at me and bringing me sweets with airplanes on their wrapping. The clouds were cotton, the blue tremendous, the world below the page of an atlas alive with worm-like cars, silent windows reflecting the light. Libya was coastline, on one side the relentless yellow desert stretching into Africa, on the other the foam-sprinkled and curling royal blue of my childhood Mediterranean.

★

When we landed in Cairo International Airport, my hostess took me by the hand. The ladies that worked in the duty-free shops gathered around me, kissed me, then wiped their lipstick off my cheeks. Each smelled different, none like Mama. I filled my pockets with more airplane-wrapped sweets. My heart leaped when I saw Moosa, his head above the crowd, his arms waving in a half-moon. I hugged him and had to restrain myself from asking to be sent back. He shook hands with my hostess, bowing shyly. She kissed me good-bye. "When will he be flying back?" she asked. Moosa hesitated, then said, "Soon, God willing."

Cairo was green, crowded, busy with farmers' turbans and women in short French dresses. An endless labyrinth stitched with cars, the wide eyes of nervous donkeys and the cry of street peddlers: clamorous, restless and darkly jubilant. I immediately liked the city. Moosa knew it well, told me stories all the way from the airport about the different neighborhoods we passed, stopped at the famous decline at Muqatom Mountain, put the car into neutral, and I was amazed how it kept ascending. It was the only place in the world, he said, where things are pulled upward by gravity. He then stopped at a fruit-juice stand and bought me a huge glass of sugarcane juice.

★

Judge Yaseen took immediate command of my affairs. And shortly after my arrival Moosa got a job in one of the new quarries that furrowed the Egyptian desert for gravel and sand. The job seemed to suit him: stone, big tractors, jeeps, the monumental scale of the land. It also helped keep him away from his father's grip. Every few weeks he would come home for a week's rest, his hair dusty, his hands parched, his neck bronzed by the sun, and be met by Judge Yaseen's disappointed gaze, mournful that instead of following in his footsteps his eldest son was squandering his time as a quarry foreman.

My life was spent mostly with his parents. His father, the solemn judge, liked how obsessive I was about my studies and so spared no expense or effort in supporting me. He was kind, generous and often reminisced about his days in Libya. I guessed he was trying to compliment me. But Libya grew distant in the background, began to mean little. All that tied me to it were the increasingly sparse telephone calls with my parents. My accent had quickly become Cairene, and I stopped trying to adjust it when calling home. Baba, in particular, disliked this. "You have become a *foul*-eater."

I had integrated rather smoothly into my new Egyptian existence. My young age and the judge helped make this possible. His wide circle of friends and associates became mine, and those old moist-lipped Egyptian judges that used to meet on his balcony in Tripoli, all those years ago, close to our house, in the neighborhood the judge liked to call Gorgi Populi, regarded me with particular affection. Doors, in a country full of closed doors, opened effortlessly, easing my progress and my definition of myself.

What was astonishing is how free I came to feel from Libya. If one of my friends teased me about my "Bedouin origins" or about our ineffective football team, I smiled only to please them, but truly felt nothing, none of the fervor that had once caused me to cry, after six hours of watching a chess match in which a Libyan had lost to a Korean at the International Chess Championship in Moscow. Nationalism is as thin as a thread, perhaps that's why many feel it must be anxiously guarded. I neither sought nor avoided the Libyans who lived in Cairo. This even when I knew that the embassy had a file on me. I was down as an "evader" because I had not returned for military service. Then, when I became too old to be militarized but was still too young to be forgiven, another decree meant that if I were to return I would serve the same period in prison. And like all Libyans who don't return, the shadow of suspicion fell firmly on me, strengthened further by yet another decree, issued when I was fourteen, promising that all "Stray Dogs" who refused to return would be hunted down. These decrees got ever more desperate. The government's next move was to refuse my parents a visa to leave the country, holding them hostage, as it were, until the evading Stray Dog returned.

Why does our country long for us so savagely? What could we possibly give her that hasn't already been taken?

I yearned for them, my room, my workshop on the roof,

the sea, Kareem. What I missed most was the smell of our house. Once, but only once, when I was still a boy, I cried and screamed, throwing things as I had done before to stop Baba going on one of his endless business trips. Judge Yaseen reacted nobly. He simply shut the door to the room that he had given me in his house, then later sent the maid-servant in with a cold glass of sugarcane juice. I buried my face into the sharp lavender smell of the pillow, mourning the familiar: digging my face into her neck, kissing his hand.

★

Medicine became my profession. I am now a pharmacist. A concocter of remedies. My relationship to illness is purely formulaic. I stand in a white coat most of my days, behind a counter in an air-conditioned pharmacy in Cairo. It's a bit of a joke. After all the hopes of becoming an art historian like Ustath Rashid, a high-flying businessman like my father, a pianist, I became a pharmacist in a city where it is nearly im-possible to look down any of its streets without spotting at least one pharmacy's flashing sign of a serpent coiling up a Martini glass. I am fully aware of how even this choice was influenced by her, what she called her "illness" and "medi-cine," the colorless liquid supplied under the counter by the baker, still illegal in Libya. At times I wonder what Majdi the baker thinks of her now.

★

I suffer an absence, an ever-present absence, like an orphan not entirely certain of what he has missed or gained through his unchosen loss. I am both repulsed and surprised, for ex-ample, by my exaggerated sentiment when parting with peo-ple I am not intimate with, promising impossible reunions.

Egypt has not replaced Libya. Instead, there is this void, this emptiness I am trying to get at like someone frightened of the dark, searching for a match to strike. I see it in others, this emptiness. My expression shifts constantly, like that of the prostitute who waits in your car while you run across a busy road to buy a new pack of cigarettes for the night. When you walk back, ripping the cellophane, before she has time to see you, you catch sight of her, temporarily settled in another role as a sister or a wife or a friend. How readily and thinly we procure these fictional selves, deceiving the world and what we might have become if only we hadn't got in the way, if only we had waited to see what might have become of us.

24

She sometimes telephones to describe a meal she has cooked for her brothers and sister and aging parents. After Baba denounced his political convictions, or had them denounced in him, the relatives showed their approval by visiting my parents again. In fact, Mama has become the family darling, successfully matching some of my endless cousins, whose names I have never tried to remember, with suitable spouses. "The food was so delicious," she would say, "it deserved your mouth," and I would hear myself thinking, how could you possibly know what my mouth deserves?

After it became clear that the road out of Libya rarely leads back without humiliation, she began to regret sending me away, began telling me about Osama, Masoud and his brother Ali, Adnan, Kareem, that although, yes, they had to do their military service, "God was gracious enough" to end the war in time so none of them were sent to Chad. I reacted calmly to such repentance, but did feel the clasp of anger around my neck. "It was the best thing you ever did, sending me away," I would say, knowing full well that the line was tapped, that my words would be diligently recorded in my file, along with the eavesdropper's comments, perhaps scribbled along the margin, kept for eternity.

I hated how her confidence plummeted with time, how she reflected on the past and hunched in front of it in regret. I wanted her certainty back, even that ruthless, steely certainty that made her send me away against her husband's reservations and her only son's plea.

★

In 1979, a few days after I was sent to Cairo, the entire Libyan population was given three days to deposit liquid assets into the National Bank. The national currency had been redesigned, they were told, to celebrate the revolution's tenth anniversary. People deposited pockets of coins and others suitcases of notes and some a truckful of money only to be told afterward that individual bank withdrawals would be limited to one thousand dinars annually. My parents were badly affected by this, their monthly output alone was in excess of that amount. The following year, private savings accounts, which were effectively what most accounts had become, were eliminated, and my parents watched their money vanish "like salt in water." This meant that even when they were allowed to, during the first years of my stay in Cairo, my parents couldn't afford to visit; and, more crucially, the cost of my education and living couldn't be met and therefore had to be endured in total by Judge Yaseen, who was amiable about the whole thing. "You and I are one, man. Suleiman is like my own," he said to my father over the telephone.

Father was left with no choice but to seek employment. He got a job as a "machine operator" in one of the nationalized factories. It was a pasta factory. Both he and Mother seemed to treat this as a novelty in the beginning, and I was encouraged by their high spirits, and smiled too when I received a bag of pasta with his beautiful handwriting on the plastic packing: "A souvenir," then in brackets, "My machine seals the packing." I admired how well he seemed to accept this mean fate. He seemed to find some pleasure in it, liked the hours, Mother said, the early start and the noon end. She said he had started translating a book from the Italian.

"Niccolò Machiavelli's *Discorsi sopra la prima deca di Tito Livio*," he told me proudly, clearly enjoying the *r*'s and the *o*'s. "Only *Principe* and *Dell'arte della guerra*," he went on, "exist in acceptable Arabic translations. But I feel *Discorsi* sets the record straight about this misunderstood philosopher. He wrote it eighteen years after *Principe*. He was sixty-two, so much wiser, and didn't have the Medici breathing down his neck." He paused. I could hear her voice in the background. "Your mother has no idea what I am talking about," he said, the smile clear in his voice. I could hear her laughing. "Anyway," he said, "helps keep the Italian alive."

But recently, fifteen years from when I was sent away, in May of this year, 1994, Baba was arrested. There was confusion at first; rumors of embezzlement had surfaced. How embezzlement could be possible from the position of machine operator I'll never know. Then the truth emerged. After fifteen years of being a machine operator in the packing department of a pasta factory, Baba decided to take his book with him one day and read from it to his fellow factory workers, not *Discorsi*, but *Democracy Now*, the book I had rescued from the fire. Mother was furious.

"How could he have done such a thing?" she said over the telephone. "Has your father forgotten what kind of country we live in? And where did he find this book? Didn't we burn it?"

I knew it was best to say nothing, but the temptation to inform our eavesdropper was too great. "I saved it," I said. After a vacuous silence she yelled, like a child pleading, "Why? Slooma, why?" and I, fully aware that the telephone line was tapped, that what we were having was a three-way conversation with the third party silent, said, "It's my book, I am to blame, Baba never believed in such ideas," knowing that such words rescue no one but only implicate.

There was indeed an element of intrigue and madness in the way Father had behaved. He, more than most, must have known that "walls have ears," that informing on your fellow citizens is Libya's national sport, that the Medici were breathing down all necks. Had he, at the young age of forty-eight, gone senile? Had he managed to delude himself that he could still change things? Had he come to prefer death over slavery, unlike my Scheherazade, refusing to live under the sword?

I began to get telephone calls from her brothers, the "High Council," urging me to return, promising I would be spared the Evader's prison sentence, that they would see to it that "friends in high places" would doctor my file, cross out the words "Stray Dog." I began to consider this, consider it seriously. Particularly because Mother began to sound depressed, recalling all the missed opportunities: the education and careers she might have had. Loneliness seemed to remind her of all the things she had missed. Then once I telephoned and got that old voice, altered, her words lagging behind, that same nervous giggle that was somewhere between laughter and crying. I felt the room turn around me. I hung up. When she called back the following morning and I heard her voice, anxious, genuinely confused, I hung up again. The messages, the countless messages she left I erased without listening to their content. She didn't go as far as calling Judge Yaseen, or asking one of her brothers or father to call me.

Then the most extraordinary thing happened. I received a letter from Kareem. The stamp told me that it was from Libya. It seemed a cruel intrusion into the life I was making in Cairo, where I was handsome and independent enough to be surrounded by all the illusions of immortality, a desire very similar to wanting to be free of the past. The delicate, nervous handwriting, the letters modestly inverted, scratched with a consistently needle-sharp pencil, no doubt rhythmically turned in the fingers with an obsessive diligence for evenness and consistency, made me long for my childhood friend.

> *Dear Suleiman,*
> *For a long time your mother refused to give me your address. She offered several reasons, none of them convincing. Once she said that the judge didn't allow you to receive letters. "Give it to me anyway," I said, "I won't write, I'll visit instead." "Stop pestering me, Kareem, I don't want you to distract him," she said. So I stopped asking after that and was content only with hearing from her that you are well. I miss you, dear friend. And now I am sorry that when I have finally managed to write it's to inform you of news that fills my heart with sorrow.*
> *Your mother is unwell. She has not left your house for weeks. I visit her—don't worry, what's missing from her life is only to see you, I am making sure she needs for*

*nothing. Stacked on her bedside table are sealed envelopes
addressed to you. At first she would hide them from me,
but lately she has been so unwell. Sometimes she can't
even recognize me, thinks I am you. I took the opportunity and copied your address. I hope this reaches you. I
hope that it finds you well. I hope you still remember me.*

*In this country we don't understand the illnesses of
the heart. What I tell her, no matter how sweet, I am sure
tastes as bland as cotton wool. She needs you. Call her
soon.*
Your friend and brother,
Kareem

I wanted to know his news, what had become of him and
the rest of the boys. I wanted to know if he still remembered
my betrayal. I had heard from Mama that Kareem and
Auntie Salma, afraid of losing their house after Qaddafi decreed that anyone had the right to claim a vacant property
as their own, had returned from Benghazi to Mulberry
Street. Other than this I knew nothing of what Kareem's life
was like. I detested how she and her past, how her "illness"
injected the world with so much urgency that not even my
childhood friend and I had time to reminisce. And so even
this letter, with its careful and delicate handwriting, that had
come through against her will, I refused to respond to.

Then, on the first of September, an amnesty was announced in commemoration of the revolution that had orig-
inally placed the now pardoned behind bars. Father was a
beneficiary of this warped mercy, and Mother returned to her
sober self, busy again with her duties, with the marriage she
had resisted and now could not live without. He remained at
home and would sometimes telephone me, saying, "I just

wanted to hear your voice," and so I talked for long stretches of time to satisfy this desire. When he handed the receiver to her I noticed a peculiar aloofness enter my voice. She tried, always, to break the distance, to bring me back, to have me speak with love.

One month after his release, and, cruelly, a few days after the ban on Libyans traveling abroad had been lifted—making me at once jubilant and nervous at the thought of seeing them again—my father died.

★

It has been forty days now. Today the mourners, according to Libyan custom, can remove their black clothes, play music, whistle and sing to themselves as they paint their eyes in the mirror.

He died two deaths, both existing simultaneously in my heart. The first was according to my mother.

"Heart attack, in the night, during sleep," she said, and, to comfort me, added, "He died painlessly," whatever that means.

I could hear in the background the piercing voice of Sheikh Mustafa, the house full of mourners. I didn't ask if she was beside him when it happened, or if his snoring had driven her to the sofa. I didn't ask what were his last words. Nothing seemed to matter. He was dead.

Then she seemed distracted. She wanted to get off the telephone, attend to the countless people who had come to offer their commiseration. "Everything is fine," she said hastily. "Don't worry, habibi. We'll speak more later, OK?"

How silly it is to still be the boy away, the one who interrupts the movement of life, and who always needs to be kept up with the news, actively included.

"Siham," she called. "You remember Siham, Nasser's sister? Here, she wants to speak to you," and Siham's voice came on, shy, excited, intrigued.

"Suleiman? Hi, how are you, do you remember me?"

"Yes . . . Of course," I said, astonished at how vividly I could recall her chestnut hair, her soft virgin lips, and confused also by the heat that was, after all of these years, blushing my cheeks. "How are you?"

"I am engaged," she said happily.

I was relieved she didn't utter the usual platitudes, hoping that God would compensate me for my loss. I didn't want to ask about her old father, I was sure he was either dead or dying. "How's Nasser?"

"He's very well, very well," she said excitedly. That mysterious melancholy she had as a child seemed to have been replaced with a lightness, a sparkling keen curiosity. "In India," she said, relishing the novelty.

"India?" I said, unable to conceal that amazement felt by Libyans living abroad when they hear that a compatriot has managed to pass through the gate, been miraculously exempt from the endless restrictions and decrees, feeling both a sense of triumph, in knowing that there still exists a thread connecting their country to the rest of the world, and jealousy, at not being permitted to return. "What is he doing there?"

"He's Cultural Attaché at our embassy," she said proudly.

Nasser must have been forgiven. No doubt a beneficiary of one of the arbitrary amnesties. Once labeled a "conspirator" and "traitor," he had become a leading member of the diplomatic community, installed in "our embassy" in one of the most illustrious countries in the world. Will he be our Octavio Paz, I wondered.

"Good," I said. "Wonderful news." Then, after an awkward pause, "Will you be visiting him?"

"Perhaps for the honeymoon," she said, laughing to someone beside her.

"Who's the lucky groom?"

"Well, I won't tell you," she said, teasingly. For a moment I had the absurd thought that it might be me, that Mother, with her new talent for matchmaking, had fixed it all up. "You know him very well," she said. "Here, he wants to talk to you. And, oh, Suleiman, I am very sorry about your father. He was such a lovely man. We have all lost a father."

"Hello? Suleiman?" a deep male voice said. "You can't recognize me? He can't recognize me," he said again to Siham. "It's me, Kareem."

It seemed I had lost my voice. Was I overcome with joy or grief? Ridiculous to feel either.

"I wrote to you. Did you not get my letter?"

From these distances only blame and regret seem possible.

"I am sorry," I said, and immediately felt the need to repeat my apology.

"May God compensate you and have mercy on Ustath Faraj," he said, and I could tell from the feeling in his voice that he meant it.

I said nothing, couldn't bring myself to say the same about his father. I felt deep gratitude and searing envy. He was there in all the ways I couldn't be. Who knows what might have become of me, of Baba, of Siham, if I'd still been there? I imagined the new couple, strolling down a beach, perhaps in Goa, perhaps in Tripoli. Then I pictured them older, living on Mulberry Street, busy with children, because children change everything, reinvent life and make black days rosy, or at least that's what I have heard people say. I doubt I will ever find out. I wanted to congratulate him, wish him a happy and prosperous life with his bride, but I felt impotent somehow. Is this some divine joke, I thought, having her marry my childhood friend; couldn't you have had her marry someone else? But it made sense, of course: Siham's brother was a friend of Kareem's father. My mother might have orchestrated the match, who knows? Perhaps Father did too, perhaps he looked after the orphaned Kareem as his own; taking care of Kareem as Judge Yaseen had taken care of me; perhaps the world is fair and balanced after all; no one gains and no one loses, or no one gains and everyone loses equally. I could see my father shaking the hand of his old clerk, the Cultural Attaché, to read the Fateha, to bless and seal the engagement. I could have given her a better life, away from the country that everyone wishes to escape. But the waters have returned and washed away the blood; everybody was getting on with their lives, busy forgetting, willing to forgive.

"How's Cairo?"

"Cairo's fine," I said, clearing my throat. "Yes. Cairo is fine, I am fine."

"Well," he said, his voice withdrawing. "Perhaps we'll come and visit you one of these days."

"Yes."

"Siham loves Cairo from all the films."

"Yes. I would like that, I would like it very much, Kareem."

★

Soon after I learned that my mother had lied. Father did die of a heart attack, but it had happened during lunch, while sipping his soup—this is the second death—at that same breakfast table in our kitchen and not "painlessly." He kicked as furiously as Ustath Rashid's legs did above the National Basketball Stadium, clawing at the table, without me, without my hands, my now grown-up arms, strong enough to lift him, to press him to my chest, to say all the meager things people say at such moments. I heard the truth of it from Uncle Khaled, the poet. Returning from the funeral, he had stopped over in Cairo before heading back to America. We had met like this before, always briefly, in transit. I sense he blames me for leaving, for abandoning my parents, but it's a sign of madness, I know, to claim to know what is in another man's heart. I never told him that it was his sister who had sent me away, because I knew what he would say, "But you have had many chances since to return," and he would be right. And so I am wary of him.

We usually meet at Groppi, the café on Talaat Harb Square, in downtown Cairo. He often needs to pass by Madbouli, the bookshop on the same square. These meetings often remind me of Mother's story of the Italian Coffee House, and, remembering her suffering, I would feel my blood pressure rise. I never ask him about his children—all with names like Ed and Amy—and he is only content with knowing if I am well. But when we embrace my eyes sting with tears.

25

It is December and the Central Bus Station in Alexandria is as busy as Mecca during the days of hajj. I sit in my car for a moment to collect my courage. I consider the option of not looking for her, of waiting here until she finds me. Then I open my door and stand beside the car.

I am twenty-four and still living in Cairo, the city she sent me to, like a faithful dog still waiting, confident that his owner will come to reclaim him. And she is finally coming. Because of the air embargo she is traveling by road. With the border controls the journey probably took twenty-four hours. She'll be tired. She'll have to stay for at least a month. One month! I wonder how it'll pass. I can't even remember her face. What if I don't recognize her?

I look down at my legs, my grown-up legs in their grown-up trousers, dark wool for the winter, ironed with a crease in the middle. You're a man, I tell myself. And she's coming to see you, to see what has become of her darling boy, her only son. How will she be? Looking old, no doubt. Veiled too. What will she think of me?

Several buses are driving in and out of the station. I have no idea which one she's on. I remain beside my car. Then I see her. She is standing next to her suitcase like a girl in the city for the first time. Not veiled. Not a gray hair on her head. I suddenly realize how young my mother is. She was twenty-four when I was sent away, the same age as I am now; fifteen when she had me, the same number of years I have spent away from her. In the end all that remains are numbers, the measurement of distances, the quantity of things. Thirty-nine. She's only thirty-nine. What is she hoping for from life now, I wonder. How fitting to see her like this in Alexandria, in the city of fallen grace. I begin to walk toward her. She hasn't seen me yet. The mother who tried to never have me, the mother who never chose it, the mother who resisted in all the ways she knew how. I wave my hand above my head, thinking of calling her, but I can't utter the word. Then suddenly it comes. "Mama," I say and say it again and again until she sees me. "Mama! Mama!" When I reach her she kisses my hands, my forehead, my cheeks, combs my hair with her fingers, straightens my collar.

ACKNOWLEDGMENTS

The Sidi Mahrez poem is taken from a book titled *Libya: The Lost Cities of the Roman Empire* by Robert Polidori, Antonino di Vita, Ginette di Vita-Evrard and Lidiano Bacchielli, published by Konemann Verlagsgesellschaft mbH, Bonner Str. 126., D-50968 Cologne, 1999.

The quotation from the Koran is taken from a translation by Muhammad Marmaduke Pickthall titled *The Meaning of the Glorious Qur'an*, published by Dar Al-Kitab Allubnani, P.O. Box 3176, Beirut, Lebanon.

The first three quotations of Salah Abd al-Sabur are taken from his poem "Night and Day"; the fourth from the poem "Tale of the Sad Minstrel." All translated from the Arabic by the author.